Unforgettable

BOOK 4 OF THE PURPLE HEARTED SERIES

FRANCES FLEUR

Blurbs

Men, in general, can go jump off a cliff. At least, that's what Daisy believes and tells herself. Daisy is not a relationship girl. She is not the sort of person to let a guy get too close. The only thing men are good for is satisfying her desires.

Her life is her job. Fuelled by making a difference her Dad would be proud of, Daisy is a paramedic and loves the thrill of the job. But a twist of the arm and an unexpected shift change, causes her to be in the wrong place at the wrong time. No one expected that one emergency call would change her life forever.

Setting herself on a different path, can she really have a chance of falling in love, or is she just kidding herself?

The story of Daisy and Taron is told from a dual POV, which can be read as a stand-alone or as a follow-on from the third book in the Purple Hearted Series.

A note from the author

Please note that this book may contain triggers.

It has underlying tones of PTSD and a chapter on sexual abuse. It also has a high content of swears and smut!

Hi everyone, I am Frances, and I love writing. I am based in Nottinghamshire, England. I have two beautiful girls, a naughty dog and my wonderful husband. I have been in Education as a TA, teacher or tutor for twelve years. When I have a spare moment, or my mind starts to wander, I quickly write/type the ideas down, as you never know when inspiration can strike to create those new characters or exciting stories. I love reading and getting lost in romance novels, but I love writing them more. I hope you enjoy reading my books, and any feedback is welcome.

Let's be friends!

Don't forget to follow me on Instagram: http://www.instagram.com/francesfleurauthor

Don't forget to follow me on Facebook: https://www.facebook.com/hbpublishinghouse

Don't forget to follow me on TikTok: https://www.tiktok.com/@hbpublishinghouse

Visit: www.hbpublishinghouse.co.uk

The Purple Hearted Series

Book 1: The First – Cora and Zach's Story – Part 1 (Released March 2023)

https://mybook.to/Vyyjlxn

Book 2: And the Second – Cora and Zach's Story – Part 2 (Released May 2023)

https://mybook.to/WLMatL

Book 3: That Day – Sophie and Oliver's Story (Released July 2023)

https://mybook.to/SxuK

Book 4: Unforgettable – Daisy and Taron's Story – Part 1 (Released October 2023)

https://mybook.to/DHStYjE

Book 5: I Have to Let You Go – Trinity and Adam's Christmas Novella (Released November 2023)

https://mybook.to/lSAYk

Book 6: Never Again – Daisy's Story – Part 2 (Released May 2024)

Contents

1. Saturday night - Daisy   1

2. The week that was - Daisy   5

3. The game - Daisy   11

4. My name is - Taron   15

5. I will wait - Daisy   16

6. It is her - Taron   23

7. Time to go home - Taron   26

8. The night out - Daisy   32

9. The dinner meeting - Taron   37

10. Dog walking days - Daisy   43

11. The hen weekend part 1 - Daisy   49

12. The hen weekend part 2 - Daisy   54

13. The wife - Taron   60

14. The night before - Daisy   65

15. The wedding morning - Daisy   69

16. The wedding afternoon - Daisy   77

17. The wedding night - Daisy   82

18. Paparazzi suck - Daisy   90

19. Paparazzi really do suck - Taron   95

20. The past, part 1 - Daisy   99

21. The past, part 2 - Daisy   105

22. Undercover - Daisy   109

23. Back to work - Daisy   115

24. I can play - Taron   120

25. The date - Daisy   125

26. You're mine - Taron   132

27. You are mine - Daisy   137

28. The morning after - Taron   141

29. The morning after - Daisy   147

30. Sister time - Daisy   154

31. Football life - Taron   159

32. I think I'm falling - Daisy   163

33. I remember - Taron   169

34. What do I do? Daisy   173

35. Chapter 35 - I have to let you go   174

Acknowledgements   176

Saturday night - Daisy

♥

DOLLY PARTON - 9 TO 5

"Please, Daisy, pleeeeeease," my coworker Jay moans at me whilst amidst a 12-hour gruelling shift. Being on-call on a Saturday night is a bitch, but I love it. There is never a dull moment working as a paramedic. The variety of people that I meet keeps it varied and exciting: the drunks; the 'I am lost because I am so drunk'; the 'I don't know how it got up there, and now it is stuck' (God rest that frozen sausage's soul) and my personal, and most recent favourite, 'I cut my finger off with a knife and I wrapped it up in tissue - can you attach it back on?' The callouts are fun and an adrenaline rush that I clearly crave.

Obviously, there are serious ones, too. Like last week, we had a call out to the centre of the city where there had been a head-on collision, it had my heart racing and the adrenaline pumping at full power. Luckily, it was only minor injuries, but I always enjoy it when I get to see the firemen do their work; men (and women) in uniform always have an air of power and sexiness to them. Or, like now, the call out to the old man who lives on his own (the house he bought with his wife over sixty years ago) with a suspected stroke.

We brought him in an hour ago and the A&E team are doing their tests. I make a mental note to check on him later to see how he is doing. He is a sweet old man with no one around, it makes me sad for him how lonely he must be. The hours are long, and the work is tiring, but it is the most rewarding and fulfilling job I could ever ask for. I have only been a paramedic for less than a year, but it is the best job I have ever had; it is the only job I have ever wanted to do.

"Please cover my shift next week," Jay continues, "it's mine and my wife's wedding anniversary. My parents have even agreed to have the kids. We never, ever, get to go out anymore. I need to get drunk and have sex with my wife. Otherwise, I will go mad!"

"Too much information, Jay," I remark whilst shovelling my pasta lunch/tea/dinner/midnight snack, whatever this is, into my mouth, failing miserably as most of it ends up on my lap. The emergency call and drop off to the local hospital means we actually can have our break in a staffroom with a hot cuppa, rather than hiding out in the van in the middle of nowhere.

"Come on, Daisy, my dick may shrivel up and die. My girls are amazing, but they are the biggest cock blocker known to all Dads, so really what I am trying to say is...pleeeeease," Jay melodramatically falls down on the sofa, lies on my legs whilst I am trying to inhale my food. I have about two minutes left until we need to be back in the ambulance and clocked in. Jay puts his hands together in prayer and flutters his eyelashes. For a forty-year-old man, he acts about twelve, but, he is such a great laugh to work with. His balding hair was shaved off in his thirties, he can grow a moustache in a day and he works out frequently. Not that you can tell much of anything when we are in our green overalls. He also likes to fart and leave the van. He does this when he knows I have to make a call to HQ and can't leave the van for a good 30 seconds.

He stinks!

But these are the random things you learn about each other when you have your work colleague as a paramedic. The hours are long and we have to work closely together. Having these random chats at 3 am in the morning helps me to stay awake. But it's also the odd things you say to one another when going to the next emergency call, just to keep you sane, calm and collected – I think if I didn't have him as my work colleague, I would go mad, his crazy personality keeps me grounded and this helps me not to take every death or incident too personally. He's like the big, goofy brother I never had! I push him off me and he rolls onto the floor and starts hitting the lino with his arms and legs like a baby having a tantrum. I laugh as I stand up and walk over to the sink, rinsing out my pot and refilling my flask with tea. "Look what you've reduced me to," he cries in a pathetically funny way as he sprawls out on the floor.

I would do a lot for Jay, I don't even mind covering his shift. That is not the problem. It's where the shift is. The London Stadium, again, is okay. It's what's there that I don't like.

FOOTBALL.

"Jay, you are covering the footie match, next week and I *really* hate them, though." I walk back over to the chair and put my coat on. I don't mind watching football with a pint. I support everyone, which is what a non-supporter would say. I have been dragged to a few matches in my time and I have enjoyed it. I like watching 22 beautifully, fit men run around in shorts and getting sweaty.

But working on call at a match is totally different. It's intense and really overwhelming. The place is absolutely jam-packed with so many supporters it's intimidating. Most of the time when I have been on-call there, it hasn't been too bad when dealing with the public, it's either small things such as a fall up the stairs or a cut. What bothers me, is the loudness, the drunkenness, the dirty and sweary songs and a whole lot of testosterone that I personally struggle with. That is what I want to avoid at all costs.

"I will owe you, so big, I will cover any of your shifts you ask," he gets down on his knees, grovelling, hands clasped together in a mercy prayer again. "I know you hate them, but think of it as you get to watch the match," he whines, "it isn't even one of the big last games where it's playoffs or who's getting relegated. So, it won't be too many drunks or fights. It will be a nice, calm game." Jay puts up his three fingers in salute of Scout's honour. "I promise to you, my dearest Daisy Wilkinson, that when you are on my watch, you will never have to be on-call for a football match again this year."

Now he has my attention.

"Really?" I ask, raising my eyebrows in surprise. He puts out his little finger in a curve.

"I pinky promise, Daisy Doo!" I snicker and put my finger out and curve it into his, to which we shake awkwardly. He pulls me into a quick hug. "Thank you," he grabs his phone from his pocket and voice notes his wife. "Night out and sexing you up is a go, I repeat, sex is a go. Get shaved and double up on contraception because you, wife, are going to be ruined." He laughs and puts his phone away.

"I think I am the one mentally ruined now," I mutter—too much imagery for 11 p.m. My walkie cackles to life, indicating that our break is now over and a new emergency call is coming through. Back to the grind, I welcome my bed in T-minus 8 hours!

The week that was - Daisy

LYKKE LI – SEX MONEY FEELINGS DIE

I roll over and groan. Last night had been a heavy one and man, was I paying the price right now. It was a belated birthday night out with friends from university and some people from work came too. We had gone out for a tapas dinner and drinks, many, many drinks. We all ended up in a hot new club in Leicester Square. There were many shots consumed and some very bad karaoke, even dancing – it was awesome! However, those extra shots last night seemed like the best idea, yet this morning feels like the worst idea I have ever concocted.

I am never drinking again!

My head feels like I have a pneumatic drill piercing through my skull and clearly, at twenty-four years of age, I still don't know my limits. I hadn't seen my friends altogether pretty much since we graduated from Ipswich University. We all shot off in different directions last year, but we stayed close thanks to group texts, monthly meets and lots of video calls. Our conversations are always ranting about something or other, how (most) men are dickheads or who had the worst call out or patient that day. My four years studying paramedic science were some of the best years of my life, but not for the reasons you would think - which is an odd thing to say. But when you know something is good in your life, you have to grab onto it with both hands, and I did just that.

All I ever wanted to do was escape my home town. I always felt trapped and alone, especially after Dad died. When I finally left home and went to university, I was ready for a fresh start. At university, I found myself as a person, and I learned who I was. University made me whole again. Leaving home, school and those shitty memories behind was the best thing I ever did and I will never return there, not for a million pounds. No one and nothing will ever make me go back there.

Rant over!

I hear the toilet flush, and Daniel, my on-off boyfriend, friends with benefits, the man who takes care of my needs - whatever he is, opens the bathroom door with his boxers on. His almost-there six-pack and slender body were good to eye over and I remember all the dirty things we did last night, which makes me smile and my lady bits start to wake up. Until my hangover says hello again and puts that fire out quickly.

"Morning, sleepy head," he smirks playfully.

"Morning," my voice sounds horse and I groan again, pulling the quilt over my head. I don't want to be awake at this hour, but I know Daniel is on shift at 7 am this morning and I had practically begged him to come home last night in my drunken horny state. Drunk sex was always a bit wilder with Daniel, and I liked that. I feel the bed dip as he climbs back into bed with me and under the quilt.

"I had fun last night," he gently places a kiss on my lips and I open one eye at him; the ridiculousness of us both hiding under the bed in my apartment, as if we have been naughty teenagers, makes me giggle. But this is my place and no one else is here. Then I feel another dip in the bed. Oh, apart from Kevin, my ridiculous, awesome border collie – don't judge; human names for dogs are the best. As if on cue, he starts to bark.

"Oh my gosh, Kevin, not so loud," I croak out. I hear Kevin jump back off the bed, growl, shake and patter down the hall.

"That bloody dog got in the bed again last night," he pouts.

I laugh. "I like him in the bed." He frowns and gets out of bed, pulling the quilt off himself and me. I snatch it back.

"You're not a dog, Daisy. He needs to sleep in his own bed, or at least on the floor." I watch him as he takes off his boxers and grabs a towel from the cupboard. His words annoy me. Kevin is my baby and he will sleep wherever I want him to. It is not my fault that Daniel is not a dog person.

Who's not a dog person?

I remember someone saying you can tell how nice a person is by the way they react to your dog. Is this a bad sign that he doesn't even like dogs?

Daniel is a junior doctor; we met at the hospital. He has the generic 'boyband' face of men that I like. The face with soft features, a cute smile, dazzling green eyes and dark spikey hair. He is my type - if I have one. Although, I have never had a boyfriend, and Daniel will never be that either. That sounds so much harsher than I intended it to, but it is true, we have an agreement of sorts. He is nice to look at, to fuck, to chat and have a laugh with, but that's it. It isn't that he's bad-boyfriend material. It's me; I am bad girlfriend material. I hate the thought of getting too close to someone, to be that open, that intimate with one person, then they could leave and who wants that kind of heartache? Not me! So, I don't want to be in a committed relationship, *ever*.

I am a strong, independent woman and I have been for a while; being on my own and counting on myself is all that I am bothered about. I like my life as it is. I don't want or need a man to dictate my life or have to rely on anyone. Cora, my sister, moans at me all the time, saying that I have had attachment issues since Dad died. He died nearly seven years ago. Can I still have attachment issues from that? Maybe. To be honest, when Dad died, I truly lost myself for years.

Some of what Cora says is probably true, she is older and wiser...

However, if this is the way I feel comfortable in my life now, I say fuck them all, literally. I am happy with my setup and I am the one who has to live with myself.

Daniel pulls the quilt off again and starts to pull me off the bed.

"Daniel!" I scream. He lets go and laughs.

"Come in the shower with me," he waggles his eyebrows and starts to pull off my silk nightie. As much as I want to say no, the impending doom of the match this afternoon smacks me in the face. I already feel stressed; Daniel is already naked, so some sexual relief and release might help to ease the tension. Plus, whilst I am there at the game, I can think of the great sex I am about to have - that might help get me through the match, too.

I curse Jay and his sweet-talking me to take his shift at the football ground already.

Daniel walks over into the ensuite and turns the shower on, he comes back to the doorway with a cheeky smile and drops his towel, showing me what he wants and how ready he is for me. "I've got to leave soon and I am on nights for the next ten days. I need you, now!"

I giggle at his demands and follow him into the shower. The warm water makes my muscles relax instantly and my headache eases slightly. He kisses me deeply and I groan into his mouth; his tongue tastes like mint toothpaste and mine probably tastes like sandpaper and last night's drinks, but who gives a crap! The water rains down on us and I am glad right now that I purchased a steam shower cabin, the one with all the fancy sprays and buttons that just make me want to sleep in it. Probably not a great idea to sleep in it; knowing me I would accidentally drown myself in it! Daniel gets down on his knees, nipping and kissing my breasts, palming them with his hands whilst his other hand sweeps down to my lady area, making me moan slightly. He knows how to get me turned on quickly!

He licks, kisses and sucks at my labia and it sounds horrible, but I have had better. I really have tried to direct him in this area, but he seems to have only taken some of my advice on board, or maybe I am just particular on how I like to get off, but he never quite gets me there, but this is definitely a nice warm up. Good job his dick is massive and he knows how to use it; he has big dick energy, always ready for some sex! He comes back up, looking proud of himself and I'm not even in the mood to be nice.

"Just fuck me, Daniel," I say. He smirks, his eyes hooded. He turns me around, holding me close whilst playing with my breasts and kissing my back. The spray of the water is going all over my face and in my eyes. I manoeuvre my bent-over position to the side, putting my hands flat, in anticipation, on the tiled wall as I hear him unravel the condom. He is in me within moments, the burn, the stretch, is fantastic and I can't help but cry out with joy.

"You always feel amazing, Daisy," he starts off at a slow pace, but I am pushing back to get him as deep as possible and he groans in delight. I pick up the pace, faster, harder, he feels so good inside me. He needs to fuck this hangover out of me, or I am going to be grumpy all day.

He moves his hand around and gently massages my clit, I push his hand down harder for pressure as he takes the hint and starts his relentless rhythm. I love fast, morning sex! Then I feel him getting harder and deeper; I know he is close and that thought is enough to push me over the edge. My orgasm explodes as I moan with pleasure. He knows my tell signs and that pushes him over the edge, too, groaning and mumbling about how sexy I am. He holds me for a few moments as we both get our bearings; he pulls out and throws the condom over into the sink. I want to moan at him for being disgusting, but I am still riding my orgasm high. He kisses me softly on the lips. He grabs his penis and starts washing it. I grab some shower gel, knowing sexy times are over, soap myself up and rinse off, but that's when I see it, the yellow stream in the water.

"Daniel, are you weeing in my shower?" I ask with a high-pitched question that I already know the answer to but hope it's not true.

"Yeah, so? Everyone does it!" I literally jump out of the shower. Guess I'm going to be bleaching the bathroom today!

"Daniel, that's fucking disgusting," he looks at me like he hasn't done anything wrong. I grab my towel from the radiator and dry myself quickly, grab some tissue, put it over the condom and put it in the bin. I pull on my dressing gown, trying not to lose my shit with Daniel and make my way to the kitchen in desperate need of toast and coffee. Kevin is giving me the sad eyes that I haven't let him out yet. I stroke his back, "Five minutes, boy, let me line my stomach with food, first." I make toast and coffee and see Cora, my sister, has sent me several text messages of shit about what she wants to happen on her hen night in a few months' time. Thank goodness for Pinterest and sharing boards, so I know exactly what she needs, as I don't want to get this wrong for her. I shoot her a quick text.

"All over it, sister, chat later," that should keep her satisfied for a few hours. I grab the jam and my mouth is watering at the smell of food; I smother loads of it over the toast. I pour the coffee and sit down at the kitchen table. Daniel emerges from the bedroom dressed in his scrubs and I am unsure whether to let out my inner demon at him for the bathroom incident or let it slide. He walks over, gives me his lazy grin, steals the toast from my plate, takes a big gulp of my coffee and kisses me on the head.

"See you soon," he grabs his bag from the sofa and he's out the door. Kevin barks at his departure.

"I was thinking the same thing, Kevin," I sigh as I put some more toast on. I hate it when I'm satisfied and angry at the same time; it sends shitty weird messages to my brain.

The game - Daisy

EVANESCENCE - BRING ME TO LIFE

Ninety-thousand people are here at London Stadium. Ninety-thousand. I wish I had ninety-thousand pounds and then I could be on holiday, instead of here, freezing my boobs off. I look around, and I really should appreciate how magnificent it really is, also how worrying it is that so many people can cram into one stadium. Each section is taken by a sea of jumping people and the roar of the fans is deafening.

Today, I hate football.

I mean that with the nicest sincerity, but this shift is a bag of shit. I've taken to standing near one of the exits on the side of the football pitch. Not sure if that is to watch the game, or, easy access to the pitch and lower stands, or, that once this shift is over, I can run out the exit, far from here and be free. But I take stock and see that there is a paramedic for each corner. I hope that it is a straightforward match; no one pisses on someone else or punches the crap out of them for liking the wrong team. I recheck my watch, only another ten minutes until half-time; then I can walk around and maybe grab a cuppa; I still feel like dog shit from last night. Not even the quick, sexy times with Daniel, that greasy fry up for lunch with my friends, the walk or licks from Kevin helped.

I still want to vomit my guts up or shit my pants; both are very debatable right now. I pull my work jacket down a bit and take a deep breath. Maybe

I need a paramedic to save me, hook me up to a saline drip and send me off on a stretcher, feign a faint or a stomach bug.

Real professional, Daisy!

There's commotion out of the corner of my eye, it looks like one of the players got tackled, badly, but he's not getting up. I don't move right away. This happens all the time; Cora and I always have a good laugh at the tackles where they go down and look like they've had their leg snapped in half, only to be up again in thirty seconds trying to gain a free kick or whatever. But I keep looking because he's not getting back up, and instinct kicks in. My gut pulls at me; something doesn't feel right. I start to grab my bag and make eye contact with the player who is kneeling before him.

"Get on the pitch, get on the pitch!" he screams at me, his eyes look wild and I know right away that it is something more, something bad. I take off into a fast jog, which I always find surprising as I do not run at the best of times. I am not the fittest or skinniest of women, I have my lumps and bumps and muffin top like any respectable girl. I don't care that I am not a perfect size 8 but I am proud of who I am. Plus, exercising is not really in my vocab.

As I approach and kneel beside the player on the floor, I see him take a couple of gasps of air.

"Hello, I am Daisy. Can you tell me your name?" as I am talking, I feel his pulse. He doesn't respond to my question; then his eyes roll back into his head. I check inside his mouth to see if his airway is blocked, but it's clear.

"It's Taron," the other player shouts.

With my finger still on his pulse, I feel that now there is none. My heart is beating so loud and I feel the sweat start to trickle down my back. My training kicks in and I start to give CPR and chest compressions.

"Where's the AED? Where's the defibrillator?" I shout and as the words come out, another medical response team of paramedics is there. I continue chest compressions and the stadium crowd are silent, eerily silent. I hear a lot of people talking around me, but I am concentrating so hard on doing my job. Who knows what is being said? I briefly look up to see the defibrillator being put in between chest compressions and someone cutting his football shirt. The rest of the teammates have now formed a protective ring around him, which I appreciate as I know this fucking thing is televised. Some are looking at me for answers, some are crying, and some are praying. My adrenaline is on a high and all that creeps into my mind is Dad and his heart attack.

Shit. I push the thought away,

The electric pulse shoots out a shock onto Taron, but nothing. I carry on with my chest compressions and someone now has an airbag and puts it over his mouth, not that I minded giving him mouth-to-mouth. Even in this position, I can see that he is bloody stunning.

"Come on, Taron, come back to me," I say to no one as I continue the chest compressions. I hate this bit. "Come on, Taron, come on," tears spring to my eyes a little, and I am annoyed at getting so emotionally involved, but the cardiac arrest cases always make me feel this way.

Dad floats back into my mind again as I wipe a stray tear away. Me, running into Dad's room as I hear Cole, Dad's boyfriend, manically screaming from the next room. As I enter, Dad is laid back on the bed, his eyes half open, his jaw in like a mid-yawn with drool hanging out. Cole is dialling 999 and screaming at them to come, I have never seen him so angry and irate. I straddle over Dad's body, knowing he's not breathing and start CPR. I know already his body feels cool to the touch, but I don't care. I will try anything for this to not be my reality, where he is not in it anymore. I remember the stupid advert on television on how to resuscitate a person. I start humming 'Staying Alive' to 22 beats of the fucking song with chest compressions and then mouth to mouth. I do it again, and again, and again, for twenty minutes until the ambulance arrives. At this point, I am in a manic madness of screaming at them to bring Dad back, of feeling so alone, of knowing my life is going to change and there is not one fucking thing I can do about it. Because he's dead, he's dead, and he's never coming back.

I pull myself from my melancholy thoughts. It's odd how my brain likes to remember the shitty bits. The defibrillator is charged and ready again; another shock goes through to Taron's chest. I hear a short intake of breath and Taron's head lolls to the side a bit. "Thank fuck," I whisper. He groans and his eyes flutter open a little. "Taron, can you hear me?" I ask over his face. His eyes are a startling blue, they focus on me for a moment as I shine a small light into his eyes.

"Yes," he hoarsely whispers, "I hear you." He lifts his hand up and caresses my cheek, I instinctively hold his cold hand there. "Are you an angel?" he asks. I smile at him in relief and wipe away another stray tear.

"Today, maybe I am," I whisper back.

The medic response team are in full form now, and I stand up and take a step back so that they can take over. One of the players hugs me and I realise that I am shaking.

"Thank you," he whispers in my ear. I pat his back in response, and I look up to the sky as I walk away.

"Thanks, Dad," I whisper. Relief consumes my body as I make my way off the pitch.

I don't need a cuppa anymore, now I need a shot of vodka.

My name is - Taron

SYML – WHERE'S MY LOVE

I hear her voice like an angel.

"Come back to me, come back to me, Taron..." her voice calls to me, soothing my soul. I could listen to her all day.

Who's Taron?

My brain stings, my head feels heavy, and my throat feels scratchy and dry. I struggle to open my eyes as if they have been fused shut. I hear mumbling in the distance and the consistent beep.

There's an overwhelming smell of bleach that makes me want to vomit; my chest feels heavy, but my head feels heavier.

I want to go back to where that voice is. Who is that voice?

Sleep calls me, pulling me back under, which I welcome.

I will wait - Daisy

SOFIA CARSON - COME BACK HOME

It had been over a week since saving Taron's life. His incident was all over the news, I couldn't escape it. Everyone was talking about it. It had been reported that he had a cardiac arrest and, through several days of scans and heart examinations, the doctors had decided that Taron would have an operation for an ICD. From their investigations, it wasn't a full-on heart attack, thankfully. His heart had stopped working because the blood had stopped pumping around his body as it should. So, this ICD, which is a small device, was inserted into his heart, which would then regulate any abnormal heart rhythms and detect any rhythm disturbances. It can then send electric impulses to correct the dangerous patterns and obviously, a cardiac arrest is slim to none to happen again.

I was so relieved when I heard the news, which was surprising.

Taron is at the London Chest Hospital, not a hospital I normally went to when on duty, but I knew a few people who worked there. I knew he was in the best place in England to get treatment, but I still felt restless. His surgery happened four days ago. I was told that the surgery had gone well. I checked in daily with the doctors on his progress, letting them know I was the first responder, so they were happy to give updates, rather than think I was being obsessive about it – which I am. He was doing really well; he was recovering well.

That's what they said about Dad, though, remember? Dad was really in my thoughts at the moment, I kept dreaming of Dad and Taron. I felt tearful for small reasons; it is really getting to me. I felt terrible. I spoke to Cora about how I was feeling about Dad and Taron, she seemed empathetic. My sister and I will share this bond for life, of losing a parent, it is what makes us so close. It was nice to say my thoughts out loud about Dad and definitely about Taron, as I felt I was going a bit crazy. Sometimes, verbalising a problem helps my brain to understand it better.

But I get it, I really do. Taron had thrown me into a bit of a weird funk, I had saved Taron, but why couldn't I save Dad? I couldn't save Dad. The paramedics who were on the scene told me I did everything right, but he still died. Why didn't I hear him when he needed me most? Did he cry out alone on his bed even though I was in the next room? That thought alone makes me still feel so helpless. I have had many years of counselling over this and I have made peace with myself, sort of. But that was always the fucked-up thing about it all. Could I have saved him if we were in the same room?

Deep breaths, Daisy.

The itch to check on Taron is unbelievable, it was like an invisible pull, a wanting, I couldn't place. Maybe I can blame this feeling on Dad, too? My mind wouldn't rest. I don't know if it was because he had a cardiac arrest or that I couldn't save Dad, but I had saved Taron, or if I was just a caring medical practitioner, but there are so many thoughts in my head, I couldn't get a grasp on any of them. Personally, I think it is because he is drop-dead gorgeous – no pun intended. Whatever it was, by the end of week 2, I decided to give in to temptation and go and see him.

I felt oddly nervous, which was weird because I am never nervous – nerves of steal, me. I walk past his private room first and glance in. He is sitting up reading, wearing glasses.

Jesus, he is a beautiful man.

I cannot see anyone inside the room with him, which makes me a little excited, so I walk passed again just to double-check.

Nope, no one. Then, as I walk past again, he calls out.

"Are you going to keep walking past and glancing in, or, do you need to talk to me?" His voice rumbles at me.

Busted.

I smooth down my dress, wiping away the clamminess I feel in my palms, clear my throat and enter the room. His room has many flowers, balloons and get-well cards. He is wearing a loose shirt, with his thick muscles and interweaving tattoos down his arm and baggy trousers. His hair is all curly and messy and I wondered for a moment how it would feel under my fingers. Even in his state of 'I nearly died', he is fricking oozing gorgeousness. This felt so wrong to be so utterly attracted to a patient, but it felt so, so good at the same time.

"Sorry. Hi, how are you feeling?" He looks at me, totally bewildered. Shit, he doesn't know who I am, of course! "Sorry, I'm D-"

"Oh..." he interrupts and puts down what looks like a world history book. He takes off his glasses and sits up from the bed. "It's you."

"Yes, it is," I respond, surprised.

Oh, he does remember. That's a good sign.

"I can't believe you came...I am sorry. I didn't mean to turn you away," his eyes look sad and I want to go over and hold him in my arms and tell him everything will be fine.

Bloody ridiculous thought. Stop fangirling him.

"You didn't turn me away-" I add, but he interrupts again.

"Wait before you say anything else," he blows out a breath, he suddenly looks a little nervous, "the doctor said that sensations and touch help bring memories back," he looks away, embarrassed, "I always hear your voice," he admits openly and holds his hands out expectantly.

I didn't know how to respond to that confession. How does he always hear my voice? I am not that loud when I walk the hospital corridors, or am I? Jay is always moaning about what a gobshite I am, but I thought he was messing about with me.

"Please sit," he gestures to the bed. I walk over and perch next to him, he leans forward and takes my hands in his. They are soft and warm, a stark contrast to how cold they felt out on the pitch a few weeks ago. I am pleased with the touch as a shiver of small tingles floats down my arms. A reaction I have not experienced yet, and I like it. I definitely have a crush.

I like how forward he is, but I get it; it must be so confusing for him. Not only did Taron have a cardiac arrest, but to give himself extra shit, he had 'temporarily' lost his memories too. Although this can sometimes be a normal response from the body when it has had a massive blow, it is the brain trying to keep him safe. He suffered only a slight concussion when he went down on the pitch, so I know the doctors have talked about this being (hopefully) a short-term 'problem'. I heard he had also started some sort of memory counselling to jolt some memories back into him. They're saying that his memory should return any day now.

I smile at him expectantly as he searches my face. His rugged beard and curly, messy, deep brown hair make him look like a Greek god; I don't even know if he is from Greece, but he is so bloody handsome. In a library, under the history section of Greek gods, he is in there, under 'fit as fuck' Greek god! Is it bad to drool over someone who is trying to get better? Or the fact that he is my previous patient?

For him, I will make an exception.

"I heard the surgery went well," I say, trying to figure out this awkward yet exciting encounter.

"The doctor said that a few more days and I can come home." His eyes are taking in every inch of my face and I try really hard not to blush under his sexy gaze.

"That's really positive," he is now rubbing circles with his thumb on the back of my hand, and I love the closeness and the sensation of him. "Do you remember anything?" he shakes his head sadly. I go to pull my hands away, but he grasps them a little tighter as if I held all the answers.

"Wait...do you mind if I try something else?" I nod at him and he leans forwards and kisses me softly on the lips.

What the shit? I did not expect that.

Tingles shoot up and down my body and I can't help but lean into this crazy moment. His thumb is still stroking my hand and he swipes his tongue gently against my lips. I greedily open for him. We deepen the kiss and holy shit; I think it's one of the best kisses I have ever experienced. His tongue fits perfectly in mine; he tastes like mint and deliciousness. I am regretting the onion bagel I had this morning now, but who knew I was going to get tongue fucked by the sexiest football player in the world? His beard tickles my face, and I like that, too. I thought the clean-shaven was my go-to face, but I think I like the beard even better. I wonder what it would feel like with his face between my legs, a bit of rough and smooth.

Holy shit!

That thought alone is sending a lot of dirty messages down into my knickers. His kiss is soft and demanding, yet beautiful at the same time. It's one of those kisses that is hard to describe but takes your breath away and is seared into your brain for all eternity. It only lasts a few minutes but I will replay this kiss later tonight in bed. I pull back, confused and a little disappointed it ended. He smiles at me, a little embarrassed.

"What was that for?" I ask breathlessly. "Not that I am complaining."

"I thought that maybe the sensation of kissing you would bring back a memory," he admits.

Even close up, he's perfection and very distracting.

"I am not sure that would work, but okay," I try not to sound sarcastic, but I don't even understand what just happened but I want to do it again, immediately.

"Well, as my wife, I thought that it might bring back memories. You are a gorgeous woman, by the way," he gives me this lopsided smirk. His eyes look like they might devour me whole and, to be honest, I would happily let him, right here on the hospital bed. I wouldn't care who was watching. I shake the thought away.

Boundaries Daisy.

"I am not your wife," I respond, then it dawns on me. Ah, shit, he doesn't know who his wife is, and here I am turning up.

Stalker!

His frown shows deep on his perfect face. "Who are you? I don't get it. Your voice is all I remember, the first thing I remember." I stand from the bed in embarrassment, feeling the heat sweep up into my cheeks. This time, he lets me go. I think my whole face is a darker purple than Violet Bogart from Willy Wonka and The Chocolate Factory. I stick out my hand as a gesture for him to shake it. "My name is Daisy; I was the first medical response team on the pitch. I wanted to check in and see how you were doing." He looks at my hand briefly and then back to my face.

"So, not my wife, Melissa?" he asks again, shaking my hand lightly.

"No, afraid not," I say, trying to hide the disappointment.

"Oh," he continues, shaking my hand and still not letting go. His beautiful eyes stare into my brain, into my soul and all I can think about is sexing him up on the hospital bed again. Which is so wrong, but definitely something I wouldn't mind trying one day, you know, as one of my bucket lists. "Well, this situation stinks," he admits.

It is her - Taron

RuTH B. - LoST BoY

When Daisy spoke, she was my dream come true. Literally, her voice is all I hear when I actually get some sleep, a gentle singing siren or angel that went around my brain, over and over again. I dreamt of her, she was a fuzzy image, but now she is here—no more fuzziness only full-on Daisy in the flesh. The kiss is magical, I don't remember my best kiss, but I bet it is this and even better her body is hot. She is in a sexy blue summer dress, with buttons at the front that make her tits look massive and her curvy body perfect. Her short blonde hair only brought out her deep, brown mysterious eyes like a lost puppy, but she is obviously the most fuckable person I have seen in the last few weeks.

Shut up, Taron. I think she is my type, whatever my type is.

Being in the hospital and seeing mostly these four walls apart from when I have treatment have driven me insane. I have walked this ward a million times, every hour seems like a day. Having this heart condition is utterly insane, the operation was exhausting and I have only felt more with it the last few days. It is the not remembering fuck all about my life, that is doing it for me and if they had a saying about kicking a man whilst he is down, then I would insert it here.

When I try to focus, to remember, my brain shuts down and I get these insane headaches. They last hours. Some of them have made me full-on vomit chunks. Not knowing anything or anyone makes me so confused and alone, and borderline crazy. So, to take control, I have refused any visitors or for anyone to come and see me so I can try to figure out who the hell I am. This is now day 12 of being in here and I am no closer to figuring out who I used to be or who I am now. People keep telling me who I am and it will come back and that just makes me feel angry and incredibly irritated. I saw 'me' all over the news and who I am supposed to be, but I stopped watching that almost right away, those interviews and people talking about me, messed with my head further.

I could not believe I was so famous, but finding out through television was not the answer. The whole situation is beyond frustrating so when I found out that I have a wife, I refused to see her, even though doctors said she had waited hours some days in the hope that I would let her, but I can't do it, I don't want to let her down, or myself. I think that if I was in the same position and my wife didn't recognise me, it would kill me....again.

The headaches were a bitch, some days were better than others, like a continuous fog in my head where the outlines of figures were in the distance, but I could never reach them. The daily counselling with the head trauma specialist is helping, I think, because I have started dreaming of other stuff, I think they might be memories, but as soon as I wake, they are gone becoming a distant memory that I can't quite place or Deja Vu, but I know my memories are all in there, somewhere.

I am so fucking annoyed by all these feelings that I become quite angry with myself. Did I have an anger problem? Who knows.

The only thing that did make sense is Daisy. I thought that when I heard her voice, she was my wife, that was why she was here, but she's not and I am so bloody disappointed that she isn't.

Am I supposed to feel this way? Why does it feel that we are meant to be together?

"Can I see you again?" I want to see her again, I can't help but be honest here because I don't know any other way to be.

"I don't think that is a good idea. You are married; I am so sorry, I didn't know," her voice sounds sad and genuine, I want to hold her close and never let her go. All these feelings are so confusing.

"Why did you come?" My voice sounds gruff but I am annoyed. Maybe asking questions first and ignoring twatting doctor's advice. He said that familiar interactions and sensations will bring memories back. Fuck that, I think I may have just landed myself in a whole heap of shit.

"I'm not sure anymore," she walks towards the door, "take care of yourself, Taron," then she disappears out of the door. I stare at that door for a long time. I am not sure why, hoping that she would come back, I almost feel like punching myself in the head, maybe to knock more or even less sense into it, because what I am doing was clearly not working. But one thing I was sure about is that Daisy was meant to be mine. When she left, my whole body was on fire in a good way, I felt turned on and I wanted to bury myself so deep inside Daisy it felt ridiculous.

If she isn't my wife, then who the fuck is?

Time to go home - Taron

VANCE JOY - WHO AM I

I have slept very little the last few days. It is like my brain won't switch off, or maybe it won't let me switch off as I try so fucking hard to remember my life, and it's driving me a little crazy. Okay, screw it, I feel fucking insane. I can't stand this shit, not knowing anything.

I sit and wait on the edge of the hospital bed. I find that when I sit still, it's the worst; my mind goes over everything and nothing, like missing pieces to a jigsaw puzzle. Yet, I can't see the whole picture.

I now hate jigsaw puzzles.

I pack and repack my bag as I wait for the doctor to give me the discharge papers, just to keep myself busy. Yet, even then, my mind wanders to Daisy; it always wanders to Daisy. I'm slightly sad that she didn't come back and see me, but I think I have scared her off. I half scared myself.

She kissed you back, though; that must mean something.

It shouldn't mean anything. I honestly thought she was Melissa, my wife. It's so odd to call her that, yet I don't know her face, and I have no memories of her.

Great start!

I feel oddly nervous that she is coming to 'pick' me up soon. I say that as a loose term as I have my own driver as well, apparently.

Who is my wife? Will she like me?

I have waited hours to be discharged. I'm not angry. I know they are busy, but I am itching to leave, to get home – wherever or whatever that is. I need to start on my recovery, to get my life back, to have some sort of normality. When the doctors said I could go home this morning, I was so happy. But it is now almost 3 pm and I am ready to explode. I pace the room again and then glance at the doorway.

A lady stands in the doorway, quietly assessing me. She's wearing tight jeans, heels and a loose vest top. Her auburn hair is scraped back and she has a lot of make-up on. I know it's her, it's my wife, she is waiting for the recognition. I wait for it to hit me, anything, a small memory, a feeling, but I get absolutely wank all. She must see my face fall as she mirrors my reaction. I slowly walk towards her. Maybe being close to her will help. A familiar scent, maybe, but still nothing and I feel terrible. I give her an awkward hi and a small hug. But when I hold her, my only thought is.

She's beautiful, but not 'Daisy' beautiful.

What an utter shit thing to think.

I pull back and she gives me a soft smile. I hold out my hand expectantly to her. I need the sensation, the touch, a memory. She takes my hand in hers and a bigger smile lights up her face at my gesture. When I entwine my fingers with hers, I still feel nothing and my heart sinks so far down my torso I think it might fall out my bum. There's not even a spark or a tiny flutter.

FUCK! Nothing!

Luckily, the doctor arrives shortly afterwards, breaking this awkwardness between us. I sign the discharge papers and we leave. The staff at the nurse station wish me well. I can tell you all their names, what shifts they work, how many children they have, boyfriends, girlfriends, husbands, wives, and singletons. I remember everything moving forward, but still nothing of my past memories.

Is there something wrong with me? Of course, there is!

Nevertheless, I'm so pleased to be leaving; my care has been excellent at the hospital, but my mental health, not so much. Hopefully, getting out of here will jolt my memories. As I leave the main entrance to the hospital, the media is everywhere; camera flashes go off like the broken hospital lights. People are pushing and shouting my name. I am shocked at the display. Their questions and calls seem so far away as I hear my ragged breath ringing in my ears. I am not used to this. Do I enjoy this kind of attention? My breath gets harsher and I feel as if I might pass out.

Am I having a panic attack?

Melissa holds my hand tighter, and I glance at her for answers. She looks at me as if recognising my tell-tale signs. Do I panic often? She leads me a few steps down towards what I can only describe as a very expensive car. The driver opens the passenger's door and ushers us inside. I awkwardly pull myself in, with the help of Melissa and the door slams, leaving an eerie silence. I look at Melissa expectantly and she gives me a small smile and strokes my cheek.

"It's okay, Taron," she whispers, "you never liked the press anyway," her soft words and touch are a comforting gesture that I lean into.

"That was intense," I admit as I try to get my breathing under control. Relief pours through me as the car pulls away from that madness, away from the press and the hospital.

"They'll go away soon when they find someone else to bother, and they can't get anywhere near our gated house. You've made sure of that." I breathe out another sigh of relief and close my eyes. I'm aware we are still holding hands and I like the calming effect she has on me, even if I have no idea who she is or anything about her. But I'm glad she is here with me now; the thought of facing this alone makes my skin crawl.

Why can't I remember things about her, about our life?

We sit in silence on the way back to the house, but I appreciate that she doesn't ask me any questions or try to make small talk. Her hand hasn't left mine, and I enjoy the continual soft rub of her thumb on the back of my hand.

Just like you did with Daisy a few days back.

She looks at me a few times during the journey, I meet her gaze each time she does it. We smile at one another like awkward teenagers on a first date. But it's not; apparently, we have been married for five years and together for ten. We met through social circles, and according to the media, we were so in love. Okay, I caved and got very, very bored in the hospital, so I read up on my life a few days back. They said we were the dream couple. I caved because Daisy threw me off my centre so hard, I couldn't make that mistake again. I wanted to be more prepared; I needed to know who my wife was, and yes, I may have also talked to the nurses and doctors about Daisy to find out more about her, too.

Daisy Wilkinson has worked within the East London district as a paramedic for around a year, has a dog, is always a ray of sunshine, and is a hard worker. No one had a bad word to say about her.

Why couldn't I get her off my mind? I had to, I had to forget her, as my life is with Melissa.

As the metropolitan city starts to space out and become more of the countryside, I stare out the window, enjoying the view and getting lost in my thoughts. The drive isn't as long as I anticipated and we are soon pulling into a gated entrance of what I can only describe as a mansion. My jaw hits the floor whilst Melissa chuckles.

"It is a bit big, isn't it? I told you it was when we purchased it, but you wouldn't have it any other way. You are a stubborn little git sometimes," I look into her eyes and see love and warmth, but my mind fills with sadness. I have nothing to give back to her.

Yet.

We pull up to the entrance, and, the driver opens the door. Melissa gets out and then comes and helps me out of the car. The funny thing is, I am okay moving about, slowly walking and getting around. I find that it's the smaller movements that hurt and pull on my chest, like getting in and out of cars or in and out of bed. It's the small turns that snag at my stitches or give me what I can only describe as heartburn - if that's what it is. I have successfully attempted gentle movements up and down a small flight of stairs, which I was pleased about. It's all small steps to make the big things happen.

I am greeted at the door by what Melissa says is the housekeeper, and we also have a cook, cleaner and even a gardener. She also informs me that my personal trainer is in tomorrow to start my rehab programme and that my PA will come by tomorrow, too.

I am overwhelmed by it all.

I take all of the house in: the warm colours, the massive kitchen, lounge, media room, gym area, pool, and the six bedrooms (all en suite). I hate the fact that she has to show me around my own home. I look at all our pictures on the wall in detail, with friends, family, holidays, and football achievements. Melissa explains each one with such detail, pride and patience. I can tell what an amazing woman she is. Sharing her thoughts and memories of us must be painful when I can't share the joy with her back. I feel and remember nothing.

Had Daisy broken me, but in a different way?

I fake a headache and ask if I can go for a lie-down. I really need some time alone with my thoughts, but I also didn't want to hurt Melissa's feelings by not knowing any of these memories. I could see, though, that I had failed in this matter. I know she is hurting; it's written all over her face, and I did that.

"I didn't know what you wanted to do," she admits as she loiters on the landing between the bedrooms. "I didn't want to assume, so one of the guest bedrooms has been made up for you as well," she doesn't quite meet my eyes when she says this, as if scared to hear my answer. This woman is too good to me, I nod in understanding.

"Would you be angry if I told you I needed a little space?" I only see the hurt briefly, but then she smiles warmly at me.

"No, Taron, take all the time you need. Maybe tomorrow we can look through our wedding pictures and videos and see if that helps?" she searches my eyes in hope.

"That's a great idea, Melissa, thank you," I walk through the door and shut it, then I climb slowly into bed and cry. I don't even know if I usually cry, but I don't want to look through pictures. I don't want to remember these memories if my brain doesn't want me to. I lie there for a while until the sun sets, and I fall into a restless sleep.

The last thing on my mind, as it has been since we first met.

Daisy.

The night out - Daisy

♥

PITBULL - TIME OF OUR LIVES

Two weeks since that beautiful and mind-blowing kiss with Taron and he is still on my freaking mind. I tried to fuck it out with Daniel, but for the first time in my life, it didn't seem to work. Sex wasn't the answer. In fact, it was such a bad experience, where my mind imagined Taron whilst having sex, that I faked an orgasm and that made me sad. I never thought I would be that person. I love sex. I have a healthy appetite for it, and faking that orgasm feels all kinds of wrong. However, when chatting to my sister Cora about it, she assured me it happens at some point to everyone.

Of course, it had never happened to her, with her stupid, perfect relationship with Zach. By the end of the week, I decide to end it with Daniel, saying this fuck buddy thing isn't working out anymore. He seemed to take it quite well, but I feel a bit of a mess and this is all because of sodding Taron. Taron makes me feel things I have never felt before, and that felt fucking frightening and wonderful at the same time. I want to see him again, desperately, but he has a wife, which I have to keep repeating to myself, A LOT! I am not a home wrecker and I need to stay as far away from him as possible. All these revelations and adult decisions make me feel so bloody sad.

So, I do what I always do when I am sad, I go out and get wasted because drinking solves everything, apparently. I am deciding what to wear for my night out when my phone rings and I can see from the caller ID that it's

Cora. I pop it onto video call and set it against the lamp on my bedside table so I can continue to get ready.

"Hey, sexy sister!" she beams from the phone.

"This dress," I put the red plunge mid-length to my body, "or this dress?" I swap and show my strapless black dress to my body.

"Oh, hi, Cora, how are you? Great, thanks so much for asking, Daisy. How's your week been? Pretty good. Thanks again for asking. Oh, and by the way, I texted you the other day and you *still* haven't replied, bitch." I roll my eyes, swapping the dresses again and ignoring her mimicking. She sighs, "The red one makes your boobs bigger, but the black one makes you look skinnier. What look are you going for?"

"Both," I admit.

"Then wear the purple one, that has the plunge and the skinny effect." I smile. She was right. That dress was also a great bargain in the Christmas sale. The dress has tummy and boob control contraptions that make my stomach more in shape than the bounciness it seems to have going on. Not that I'm ashamed of my body, I know I am not the size 8 model, but I did not give one shit. I am a size 16, maybe 18, depending on how my intake of food is going that week and proud. I am body confident. I pull it from my wardrobe and lie it on the bed, smoothing it out. I grab the phone and lie back on the bed.

"What's up?" I ask, her brown hair covers the screen and her green eyes drill a hole into my phone.

"Hen weekend, T-minus 7 days," she beams at me. I smile back, I cannot believe my sister is getting married in two weeks' time. "Can you drive Trinity and me up there?"

"Yes, but you better pay for petrol. It's like a three-hour drive, and money is tight at the moment."

Kevin takes that moment to come and join me on my bed for a cuddle and lick my face.

"We can sort all that out, don't worry. I just wanted to make sure that everything is ready. Do you need me to do anything?"

I roll my eyes at Cora; she has always taken the lead since we were kids and has found it hard to relinquish the small amount of control over the hen to me. "You don't need to do a thing. Everything is sorted. Sophie has been a huge help. The only thing you need to do is relax and enjoy."

I have really enjoyed organising the hen activities for Cora. She has been a great sister over the years, and I wanted to plan something special for her as a thank you, but her idea of a hen party-appropriate weekend is definitely different to mine. But she doesn't know that – yet. It's been great to have Sophie's help and nice to get to know one of Cora's friends a bit better at the same time. It's going to be so much fun and Cora is going to love it, or at least most of it. Cora seems relieved by my response and leaves me to get ready after telling me what shoes to wear with the dress. Apparently, I can't dress myself anymore, or Cora needs to have her say in everything I do!

Sister love!

A few hours later, I met the ladies from work for girl's night. I have no work tomorrow and I am living it up in Chelsea tonight. There are only three of us who could make it out, but it's still nice to natter about men, work and the in-between. The cocktails are 2-4-1 all night, and I am taking advantage of that offer because I need to get pissed and let off steam. The last four weeks have been gruelling shifts with only a day off here and there; now, I have a full-on weekend off.

Living the dream!

We end up at this awesome club. The music is a classic mix of 90's nostalgia, with songs playing from the Backstreet Boys era, and that's my kind of vibe; I dance nonstop for hours. It's only early, not much past midnight, but I am battered, and I tell the girls I need to leave. I'm only a ten-minute walk from home, but the club is stuffy and is making me want to be sick, and I know a good kebab and diet coke will set me right. Plus, Kevin has been on his own for about 7 hours now so he will be sad and want a wee if he hasn't already on my rug!

Pretty pleased with my coherent thinking to say how much alcohol I have ingested this evening.

I kiss the girls goodbye and promise to text them when I get home. I will see them around lunchtime tomorrow (or later today) for a greasy fry-up. They don't seem too upset when I leave the club. They seem as battered as me. I walk down the steps and sway my way along the street; the kebab shop is not far. Is it shameful to say they know me? I'm a regular. What can I say?

"Daisy!" I hear someone shout. I quicken my steps; it's a male voice and I have very limited male friends. This is not one I recognise. I look ahead, not daring to look behind me. I can see the neon lights of Leeroy's Kebab House from here. It's dark and quiet on the road I am walking up, plus there doesn't seem to be many people around.

Shit.

My heart starts to go into overdrive. "Daisy!" The voice is closer now—double shit. I can't run in these heels and being this drunk as well, I will probably fall flat on my face whilst landing in a pile of my own vomit. Okay, make a plan quick, Daisy, the heavy footsteps are approaching - shoes off, throw at the perpetrator and run to Leeroy's.

1, 2, 3, GO!

I stop, pull off my heels, turn and fling it at the shouty man. He catches the first and then the second heel hits him in his face. I laugh. Good shot, Daisy. Then, the man comes into view. It's bloody sexy, Taron.

"Daisy, what the fuck?" *ohhhh it's angry Taron. I like this better.* "Yes, I am a little angry," he says. *Wait, did I say that out loud?* "You threw your fucking shoe at my face!" Another laugh bubbles in my chest and erupts out of my mouth. Sort of a 'panic, relief, and I am drunk' laugh. Not a stranger trying to kidnap me, just handsome Taron. He is so much closer; I can smell him, all manly and pine-scented. "It is not funny," he adds whilst passing back my heels. I can see I have cut him slightly on the cheek. I stare far too long as he is all shaved and looking so much more bloody beautiful.

Why are you so bloody handsome?

The dinner meeting - Taron

BLACKBEAR - IDFC

"Why are you so bloody handsome?"

Her cute remark caught me off guard, not what I was expecting her to say. I look down into her hazel eyes and play with a lock of her blonde curly hair. She closes her eyes at my touch. That's when I realise she is affected by me, the way I am by her. What the hell is going on? I can't seem to control my urges around her. I am not meant to touch her or go near her, but here we are again, paths crossing.

Do I believe in fate?

I told myself the first night that I returned home, I would never see Daisy again because I can't do this to myself, Melissa or my brain. But if the universe has other plans, and we were meant to meet, then that would be okay. And what would you know? A little over two weeks later, here she is.

This has to be a sign!

"You think I am handsome?" I joke and smirk at her. She snaps her eyes open and focuses her eyes on me, blowing out a raspberry and sticking out her tongue. The urge to place my mouth over it and suck it is ridiculous. I have spent two long weeks with my wife and felt nothing. I have had all the dinners, chats and photos and still feel absolutely diddly squat. But one minute in Daisy's company, I have a semi-lob on and want to stick my tongue so far down her throat I would probably reach her pussy.

"How are you in my head?" she cries.

"Daisy, you are doing some sort of running commentary in your head...out loud," I snigger. She looks absolutely pissed as a fart but still meets my gaze with such intensity that I can't help but fall under her hypnotic trance.

"Of course, you're handsome," she continues and sighs, "you must see it in the mirror. You are enough to bring me to my knees."

"I would like to see that," I smirk.

Why are you flirting, Taron? You are married! Fuck!

I blow out some air and step back, breaking eye contact. This woman has bewitched me.

"How are you getting home?" I ask, trying to change the subject whilst subtly adjusting my trousers.

"I am going to walk," she confesses.

I frown and assess her ability to walk home on her own, never! "Walk?" I ask.

"Don't tell me you've forgotten how to do that too?" she demands, then smacks her hands over her mouth. "Too soon?" I can't help but laugh at her dry sense of humour. There is a comfortable silence that surrounds us. Over the last few weeks, everyone I have come into contact with has tiptoed over this heart condition, this head condition. Just in case I explode, or they're worried I might have some sort of mental breakdown.

Too late there!

But Daisy just says it as it is and treats me normally. "Can I walk with you?" I ask. She mutters under her breath. "What was that?"

"I said I am capable of walking myself home. You walking me home is a bad idea," she points at me, walking backwards a little and stumbling. I grab her arm and pull her close to me.

"Why? I would say it was a great one. You shouldn't walk on your own, Daisy," I warn.

"It's not even that...it's...you are too handsome to walk me home...I...I might...we might kiss again...you're married..." she huffs out. She shrugs my arms off her shoulders, throwing her arms in the air, then drops her heels back on the floor. I pick them up, as I am not sure she even noticed.

"I am married," I agree with her. Although I often wish I wasn't.

"Still fucking married," she mumbles. I chuckle to myself as we walk along together. No way am I letting a beautiful woman like Daisy walk home on her own at this time of night. She continues to grumble as we walk along but doesn't protest again.

My recovery has been excellent. I am clear to start gentle exercises now that it has been four weeks since the operation, and if all is well and I pass my medical, I could return to playing in another three–six months, depending on training and recovery. Thank fuck it is the end of the football season. So, in theory, our first game wasn't for another ten weeks, so if I am on track, I would only miss maybe half the season. My manager has said they would bring me back on the pitch gradually, but only if I am still on target with my steps to recovery.

But I am determined to do, say and eat all the right things to make this happen. Even though I don't remember playing football, the urge to play and watch it is like a drug. When I went to the football ground last week and walked onto the pitch, it felt right. It felt like home. My whole body and mind came alive and even though there was no one in the stands, I could hear the roars and cheers echo up the plastic seats.

I felt peace.

I was worried that the manager might want to sell me to another team – the football player transfer window just opened. But he assured me that wasn't the case, in fact, he thought I was one of the best players on the team. He even said that there were a lot more opportunities for the team since my 'heart problem' had attracted more sponsorship – which meant more money, so he wasn't going to let me go, which is a great relief. I felt worried when he scheduled this dinner, so I even went in a tie and suit to look the part and feel like a power player, whatever that is. When he gave me the news, it was like music to my ears.

I know that I'm dealing with this temporary amnesia and heart condition a hell of a lot better. Taking it one day at a time, despite the headaches, things were going okay.

"Wait, stop!" Daisy shrieks. I literally want to ninja-chop someone thinking she is being attacked. She stares back at me with those beautiful puppy eyes and places her hand flat on my chest. I almost have the urge to push her down and ask for a blowy because her purple dress clings to her in all the best ways. And especially when she looks at me like this, it gives me such a rage on, I feel like I am going to explode. "Leeroy's!" she shouts.

"Leeroy's?" she does a little twirl, arms in the air, a sway of her hips and walks inside a kebab shop. I look up at the sign. "Leeroy's Kebab House."

"Leeroy!" I hear her shout, and she laughs as I enter the takeaway.

"Daisy!" someone shouts from the back, "My favourite customer," an old man with grey hair, a very large moustache and a belly emerges.

"Seems like I am your only customer tonight," she jokes.

"Yes, well, it is still early. You want your usual?" he asks.

"Yes, please," she looks back at me for a moment, "Oh no, Leeroy, make it two. I think my handsome partner here would like one, too."

"What's the usual?" I whisper whilst giving her heels back; she takes no notice of my comment. I don't even know if I like a kebab.

"Well, your boyfriend will love it!"

"I wish Leeroy, but he has a wife!" The man tuts as if being out without my wife is a bad thing, or, not being with Daisy was a bad thing. Who knew? She's going on about what happened to me. Hearing her relay the story, even the kiss we shared, makes me feel embarrassed and a little hurt. I want to leave and go home. But I am a man of my morals, I think, and I have to walk her home. She's drunk and should not be left on her own. Leeroy loads up the pitta bread with what can only be described as dog meat and a rainbow of sauces and salad. After dragging Daisy from the kebab shop and a lot more tutting and shaking of his head from Leeroy, we are back on the slow walk to her place, wherever she lives.

It turns out that a kebab is lovely, and the way Daisy devours her food makes me turned on all over again; she's licking and moaning into that kebab that I nearly walk off. That woman is unbelievably sexy. I don't think she even realises what she's doing.

By the time we arrive at her apartment building, we have both scoffed the food and Daisy seems to be less in a rage.

"This is me," she stops outside a low-rise building. She fishes her keys out of her bag and jangles them at me. I notice that she has sauce over her face and honestly, I would happily lick it off her.

Married, Taron, naughty Taron!

"Daisy, you have sauce on you." She looks down at her purple dress and sighs as I now notice she has a blob of ketchup there too.

"Shit, that better come out," she licks her thumb and starts rubbing on her dress, to which then I can see her nipples pebble at the contact. I need to leave. I pull the handkerchief from my pocket, lift her chin up gently with my hand and wipe the side of her mouth and cheek. She closes her eyes at the contact and lets out a low moan.

"Fucking hell, Daisy, you make this really hard." She opens her eyes and stares at me. I want to kiss her so much. The last time was fucking beautiful, but I can't kiss her. I have a wife.

Who you don't remember.

We stare at each other a beat too long and I know the tension between us is thick. I feel the pull radiate up and down my body like warm liquid. We both want to kiss each other. The attraction is undeniable. I start to lean closer, unable to resist, but she clears her throat and I pause.

"Who has a handkerchief in their pocket? What are you like, fifty years old?" I stifle a laugh. "Thank you for walking me home, handsome Taron," she kisses me on the cheek and leaves right away. I watch as she lets herself into the building, I stand there for a while and let the evening swirl around my brain. As I walk back down the road and call my driver to take me home, I know that one thing is certain when it comes to Daisy.

I am fucking screwed.

Dog walking days - Daisy

ARIANA GRANDE - NEEDY

A couple of days later and I am still enjoying my time off. I decided to make the most of it. It's early Sunday morning, and I head to Hampstead Heath to walk Kevin. He is restless today, I don't know whether it is the long shifts I have been taking lately and he misses me, or, if he is actually coming down with something. We walk to the top of the hill and I sit on the bench overlooking London whilst he sniffs at every blade of grass. I love this place; it's early enough that not many people are about and when you get to the top, it is worth the view. Maybe not my huffing and puffing with my non-existent exercise routine, but no one knows me here. I don't care that I look like a bag of crap this morning and that I am unfit; I hate exercise. In fact, I am allergic to it; I break out in hives or feel like I can't breathe, so walking is the best I have in me. Some people prefer the countryside walks, the hills and nature – I like that too – but what I really love is walking to the top of this hill, right here at Hampstead Heath. Overlooking the metropolitan city and its beauty in the skyscrapers and tall buildings, wondering what people are doing at this moment in time. It makes me feel so small in one respect but very appreciative in another.

And I know time can be cut short. Dad was living proof of that. He has also been on my mind a lot lately. I wonder if he would be proud of Cora and me, what he would say, if he would still be a headteacher, or if he'd married Cole. I let that thought settle for a moment in my mind. I must make a mental note to call Cole and catch up with him before the wedding. Cole is Dad's boyfriend. Was my dad's boyfriend. But he had never met anyone else since; he's still single, or so he says. Is that something a person would admit to the family after their boyfriend dies? That they had met someone else? Not sure I would have the guts.

The walk is needed to clear my head. After the month I have had, the intense relationship or run-ins with Taron have scrambled my brain. I feel so conflicted about my feelings for him, if that is what I could call them. He is married, and I have to stay away from him. The kiss we shared was an accident, and I had to put it out of my mind. He is not mine. But jeez, I want him like I have never wanted anyone else. It sends a tugging at my heart, which I just think is ridiculous. I am not a relationship person.

I suppose confessing to him how beautiful he was to his face when I was drunk the other day was an accident, too?

Shut up, brain.

I sit on the bench for far too long, that I may have caught sunburn. Even if it is only 10:30 a.m., the sun hates me regardless of the time of the day or the month of the year. Kevin is now fed up with sniffing and being in the same place for a length of time. He is racing to the tree and back to me, barking to make me hurry up.

Yeah, that ain't going to happen!

"Okay, Kevin, I get it. You are grumpy, too," I mutter. I make my way slowly down the hill, heading towards the swimming lake. I always enjoyed the swims I used to have here with Cora during the summer holidays when I used to come and stay between the breaks at university. I look at the swimmers cannonballing into the water, the laughter rippling along the slight breeze and the shimmer of the water. This is my happy, calm place.

I close my eyes and take a breather, but then I feel my skin prickle. Great, I probably have heat stroke now too. I open my eyes to call for Kevin, but that's when I see him. I almost turn and walk away, but the bugger catches my eye and the biggest smile crosses his gorgeous face.

Taron.

First, he looks like a sweaty beauty with his thick, muscly legs, his small, tight shorts and his t-shirt is off, tucked into his not-so-there shorts – I swear if he makes the wrong lunge or kicks too high, I am going to see his balls. His chest is thick with dark hair, like a forest I would happily get lost in, and running my fingers through that and across his deep, defined abs has me salivating and hitting my core. Where the hell had he been hiding that perfect body? Why didn't I notice that before? My brain is screaming at me to run, but my legs and vagina have turned to jelly, and my mouth gaped open at this Taron display of perfection.

He comes to a stop, bends down, and puts his hands on his legs to catch his breath, showing off his sexy arm tattoo. He then straightens himself—a glint in his eye.

"Daisy," he huffs out, making some sort of delicious eye contact with me.

Why is he here? How does he do that? I feel like just getting naked and jumping on his face.

"I didn't know you came here?" I snark back.

"Well, neither did I, but apparently, I used to," he responds.

"Are you still trying to see if sensations or touch help bring back your memories?"

Stop flirting with him, you mental bitch.

He smirks. Jeez, I am going to have to go ten rounds with the vibrator later just to get this ache out of my core.

He looks around and spots the lake. "Do you swim in that?" I scoff.

"Good god, no, do I look like a swimmer?" He then lazily looks me up and down, and I really bloody should have made more of an effort this morning. But it's not that 'you're a bit overweight and you look like crap' look; it's more of the 'I want to bend you over and fuck you from behind whilst I devour you' look.

Holy shit!

"I don't know what you are, Daisy," he almost growls out. I wasn't sure if that was an insult or a compliment. He looks over at the lake again and then Kevin makes an appearance, sniffing at Taron.

"Heyyy, is this your dog?" He looks at Kevin, unsure, even a little scared. Kevin is being the tart he always is and giving his best 'no one strokes me' face and 'please love me.' Which Taron awkwardly pats his head. Kevin then jumps up at his leg, giving him a collie hug and wagging his tail like Taron's the best thing ever.

Traitor. But he's not far wrong from what I am thinking, either. I wish Taron would stroke me like that, too.

"Do you like dogs?" I ask as I shoe Kevin off Taron and clip him back onto his lead.

"I don't know," he shrugs as he puts his t-shirt back on, which I am super grateful for because his face is distracting enough. I am surprised there isn't more of a scar or a mark from his operation, but with how much hair he has on his perfect chest, he could probably hide most of England in that beautiful tray of fur.

Well, let's hit the elephant in the room head-on. I thought that maybe I would have a few weeks (or never) to face Taron again, but here we are only two days later, where I nearly tongue fucked his face and continually told him how disgustingly handsome he was. Someone needs to bloody lock me up when I am drinking, clearly!

"So, erm," why the hell am I so nervous around him? I try to look cool, but Kevin is pulling me all over the place. He really does pick his time. "I want to apologise for being an absolute fart the other night. I was totally wankered, and I apologise if I made you feel uncomfortable by my runaway of a mouth."

We walk along together in a long silence. It honestly makes me want to go back to the lake and belly-flop in there just to get away from him.

"I wasn't uncomfortable," he finally says. I feel relieved at his confession but now confused over this whole interaction. "You know I never did, thank you."

I stop and look at him. "For what?"

"For what you did for me on the pitch that day. Saving my life." His intense stare gives me shivers in all the right places and this flirty banter has me so turned on that I feel all wobbly and want to sit down...on his face!

IF HE WASN'T FUCKING MARRIED!

Look away, Daisy, stop looking at his beautiful eyes, his perfect lips and how I want to just climb into his mouth and live there. My phone starts to ring, pulling us out of this hypnotic look, but you can't touch trick. I honestly feel exhausted. I am like a child in a Cadbury shop but can't touch the damn chocolate. And I frigging love chocolate.

I am relieved that the phone call interrupted us and gave me a break to look away and gain some composure. I look at my phone and see that Cora is calling and I reject her call.

"My sister," I semi-laugh and wave my phone at him. He nods. A text comes through immediately from her -

If you just rejected my call, I will come down to London and kill you myself. This is a hen night emergency. Call me back ASAP!!!!!!!!!

"I will let you get on with your day. I need to power walk another few miles anyway."

"The doctor gave the all-clear for moderate exercise?" I ask, already knowing he will say yes. I have literally obsessed over his doctor's notes to see how he has been doing. I could probably tell you when he last had his bowel movement, too, with how closely I have looked at his notes.

This is not healthy, Daisy.

"Yeah, for a few weeks and then hopefully, the all clear to start training. Although it might be longer, we shall see. One day at a time." I smile at his positivity. My phone rings again and I already know it is Cora.

"Sorry, I have to take this," he smiles.

"I will be seeing you, Daisy." He states as he speed walks away, and I can't help but stare at his bum in those shorts. I liked how that sounded out of Taron's mouth like a really sexy threat.

"I hope not," I mumble because I am really starting to struggle to control myself around him, drunk and sober.

The hen weekend part 1 - Daisy

JENNIFER LOPEZ – LET'S GET LOUD

The hen weekend is awesome. After giving Kevin fifty kisses and cuddles and dropping him off at my neighbours, I drove all the way from fricking London to this literal mansion in the Derbyshire Dales. I almost felt a butler would come out and give me some champagne and vol au vents or even a red carpet on my arrival, and I have to say my inner self was slightly disappointed it didn't happen. However, fantasy aside, it has six bedrooms, all ensuite (obviously), a dining room, a lounge, a library, a front room, an orangery (whatever the fuck that is), a swimming pool with hot tub, an entertainment centre and a cellar with so much wine in it I am tempted to sleep there. The kitchen is frigging enormous; I think that I can fit my whole apartment in it, and the garden is so big that I expect unicorns to come riding by any moment now.

They don't, by the way – another slight disappointment.

There are only four of us this weekend: my sister Cora, Sophie (Cora's friend from school), Trinity (Cora's friend from her university days) and me. Once we are all settled in, we explore each room and have a quick catch-up. Before the taxi arrives, we make Cora dress up as 'Where's Wally,' she seems pleased with the choice of outfit. It is one of the books Cora and I actually liked doing together when we were kids. I also bought her a 'Best Bitch' wedding party sash and made her wear a lot of penis-related jewellery.

She looks fantastic!

I have planned Cora a real 'treat' today. Well, actually, a bit of sisterly payback but an afternoon of fun nonetheless. We start off with an escape room, which sounds nice enough, but what she doesn't know is that I booked the 'Scare Fest' room. And she really hates scary stuff. When we were younger, we watched 'Dawn of the Dead' together and she had terrible nightmares for months. So, I convinced her, several months later, that a film with the lighter side of a zombie theme would help her get over it. I made her watch 'Shaun of the Dead,' even though that's a comedy; after she watched it, she had nightmares FOR MONTHS! Just to top it off, I purchased the book, 'Pride and Prejudice with Zombies' (Jane Austen is one of her favourite authors) thinking this was it, this would help her overcome her fear of zombies, but nope, two chapters in, NIGHTMARES. It's a long-standing running joke in the family. I think it is so funny that she is so scared of something that will never happen in reality and is made up. So, what better (to be the best sister ever) than to book her a horror escape room? Sophie is down with this; she loves horror, and Trinity is not bothered either way.

We head off into town. The taxi ride isn't that long and Cora is buzzing. I arranged this part of the hen weekend; the control freak of my sister wanted to arrange it all herself until I told her off. She had to let me do a little bit. Honestly, I am surprised she said yes. We pull up outside the escape room and I sign us all in.

"Ohhh, I am excited I have never done one of these. Which one are we doing?" Cora asks whilst scanning the board, "I hope it's the bank heist," she smiles back at us.

Yeah, just you wait and see what happens.

"The best one, obviously," trying not to give anything away because as soon as she knows which room we are doing, she is going to be pissed off and I might not get her in the room. I give the girls a friendly glare because they know she won't do it either if she realises what's in store, and they better not rat me out.

"Okay, I'm Bailey, I am your room organiser. Has anyone not done an escape room before?" Cora puts her hand up; it seems everyone else has completed an escape room in the past. But what screams more fun than being locked in a dark room, shitting yourself whilst trying to figure out a mystery.

My kind of thrill!

Bailey quickly explains that we have to work out all the clues and find the code to get out of the room within sixty minutes to win. He ushers us into the room whilst explaining the fire drill, if there is one. Also, good job that I phoned ahead and told him not to spoil the surprise. The door is locked and we are plunged into darkness. Cora is standing in front of me, and I hear her breathing becoming laboured.

"Girls? Daisy?" she grits out. "What bloody escape room have you booked out?" I can feel the fear radiating off her body already. I guide her reluctant figure into the room and it's everything and more than I expected. The portraits on the wall turn from smiling figures to skeletons, the rooms dimly lit with fake candles with cracks going down the walls. There are cobwebs, lots of cobwebs and it's really smoky with borderline sinister music.

Perfect.

I grin with pleasure and almost feel like tapping my fingers together and saying 'excellent' like Mr. Burns in The Simpsons.

"I hate horror, I'm out!" Cora shouts.

We crowd her in so she can't escape, "Cora," Sophie soothes, "It's not real, this is just for fun. We will make a horror fan of you yet," Sophie's grin is wide. I can tell she is having as much fun as me!

"Funny, you think this is bloody funny?" we all start to giggle. Even in the darkness, we can see she is angry. Really angry.

"It is pretty funny," I remark.

"Daisy, you are dead to me," she spits out.

"Here's hoping," I muse.

Throughout the 60-minute ordeal, I'm practically giddy with excitement. Bailey is a fantastic host. He even enters the room in a black cloak, scaring the crap out of all of us. But the highlight of it all is Cora. I'm not one to get high on someone else's fear, but when it is my sister, it's flipping hilarious. At one point, she is locked up in a pitch-black cupboard to which Bailey, the legend, blows air on her and lets things like fake spiders fall into that cupboard. I have never heard such loud and terrifying screams in my life, and all we did, as a sister and good friends do, is laugh. When we completed the room, Cora came out in such a bad mood that she was practically shaking with rage and tears.

"Just know, bitches, we are no longer friends," we could not help but laugh even harder. Who said hen weekends needed to be full of strippers and drunk ladies? This is, by far, the best fun I have had in ages. I even video-recorded some of Cora's breakdown and messaged it to Zach; he can thank me later.

I make it up to her with a bottomless brunch, a massive, I'm sorry (not sorry) apology with a fun quiz about all of Zach and us. I inhale as much prosecco as possible; I even nip to the bar with Trinity and we have a few cheeky shots. Then we finish the afternoon off with 'Go Ape', a fantastic outdoor adventure, where we have a set of courses to complete high up in the trees. It's lots of fun with climbing, balancing on ropes, and then down-zip wires. I was still buzzed from the alcohol. Although I did regret it later when I had to do a lot of jumping and definitely brought up sick and swallowed it – serves me right for taking that last shot.

It's always that last shot that gets me.

By the end of the afternoon, we were all exhausted. My hands are sore from all the rope holding and hanging on for dear life, my thighs are burning from all the climbing and I hadn't thought about Taron once. I am really pleased with myself.

Oh, and Cora had forgiven me.

The hen weekend part 2 - Daisy

COLDPLAY - YELLOW

I hug my cup of coffee on the decking and breathe in the morning air. I slept like a baby. Those beds are made of feathers and dreams. We had a team of people come in and make sushi last night and it was so much fun. I like the intimate setting it offers here and also the zero chance of me going out, getting wasted and making a fool of myself, or bumping into Taron. I mean, how unlucky am I? There are millions of people living in London and we see each other twice in one weekend. What are the chances of that? Zero, that is what the chances are.

Yet it happened! Bad luck is what I am putting it down to.

"You, okay?" I turn to see Cora half awake, in an avocado hoodie and flip-flops, hair all over the place, still looking amazing. She is definitely gifted in the looks department. I am gifted in the big boob and big gob department.

"Yeah, just thinking," I reply and look out onto the field again. She leans against the decking bannister.

"Taron?" she asks.

"Taron," I confirm. She sips her coffee and sighs. It was half him; I was still confused about the whole situation; the way my body felt like it was instantly ready to orgasm as soon as Taron was near, was damn right embarrassing. I have never been so sexually reactive to anyone in my life. No, the real reason I was up early was that I had a nightmare. Something I haven't seemed to have grown out of yet. I didn't get them that often, and I didn't want to admit it to my sister that I had. I knew if I did, she would be upset with me. That even after eight years since it happened – five years since I last came face to face with him, Stefan Routledge was still lurking in the dark corners of my brain, with his blue eyes staring at me, his hands brushing back his floppy brown hair, it is always the same dream. I hated it, I hated him. I could never fully run away from my past; it always pulls me back in some way or another.

"Sister, I have no words or advice for this," she continues, pulling me from my thoughts.

I scoff, "That'll be a first," she gives me a soft smile.

"True. I am one to talk about following the not-so-gracious path. But the heart wants what the heart wants."

"I still can't believe you are marrying Zach," I admit. Zach was, many years ago, Cora's A-level music teacher. They met before they knew this of one another, or so they say. But after a stop, start relationship and after Cora left school, moved and went to university. They got their shit together. Now, over seven years later, they are getting married. It is still a bit weird how their relationship came about, but he is family, and Amy (his daughter) is too. Cora loves Amy like a mother, and I treat her like a little sister. She is an amazing young lady, but the teenage-hormonal fourteen-year-old has overtaken her at the moment, so I know things are a little tense in Cora and Zach's house currently. Cora tells me often that she can't seem to do anything right with Amy at the moment.

I look at my sister and her dreamy expression. She is so in love and happy. I guess if it boils down to it all, I am a bit jealous. She's had Zach to support her through thick and thin. When I first saw them together, it was sickening how well they complemented each other. They were meant for each other. I don't believe in all that soul mates' crap, but for them, I do. They are perfect, which also makes me fucking sick to my stomach as I never want to be this reliant on another person because, if I am really honest, it scares me.

"I love him so much. Life without him is incomprehensible," I roll my eyes. "Maybe Taron is your one."

"He's bloody married, Cora; he is somebody else's one. He is not mine," I sigh, "he can't be," I whisper.

"People change, Daisy, and there is nothing you can do about that. Things happen for a reason."

"I don't believe in that shit," I sulk.

He can't be my one.

Later that afternoon, and after a cocktail-making session, I am royally smashed. It's a great place to be, an even better feeling to have, and everyone is welcome. Everything is bloody hilarious. Cora and Trinity are pretty tipsy, too. We are lying over Cora's ridiculously massive bed, eavesdropping on Sophie's conversation with her boyfriend, Oliver in the next room. She has been a bit nervous about leaving her daughter, Hope, for a weekend. Apparently, she hasn't ever done it before. Her constant check-ins, voice and video calls were a bit excessive, but whatever settles her mind, she's had a pretty shitty few years as well. It turns out that Stefan is to blame for not only my own unhappiness but the unhappiness of several girls from school and what he did to Sophie was the worst. Causing her all that pain for all those years was disgusting and made my stomach turn to even think about it. But that is her story to tell. The fact that she found happiness and with Oliver is a miracle. After all, being happy is all I ever want in life.

"I miss you," Oliver says. His voice has such a soft Scottish accent; it's sexy.

"Well, you can show me how much tomorrow," Sophie says playfully.

"Do you think they're going to have phone sex," Trinity whispers, and we all silently giggle.

"Why not now?" Oliver suggests. We all laugh again.

"Oh jeez, Sophie, can this wait until tomorrow?" Cora calls out to Sophie to which we all burst out laughing, making kissing noises, "We can hear you!"

We all laugh again, then Sophie emerges from her room a few moments later with pink cheeks, joining us on the gigantic bed that could probably sleep all of us comfortably.

"I am so pleased for you," Cora beams out, "you deserve so much happiness, Sophie."

"You know, I never did thank you both for testifying in court about Stefan," Sophie states after a few moments.

"He was a dickhead," I slur, "and I am not afraid to say out loud that I am glad he is dead. The world can rest easy."

There is an awkward silence and at that moment, I realise that I have no filter. Then Sophie lets out an uncontrollable laugh; then we are all laughing. I don't even know what for. Tears roll down my face, and I swipe them away quickly because these are not tears of happiness. These are tears of pain whenever I hear that dickhead's name.

"So, have you met someone?" Trinity asks me, I am grateful for the conversation change. She probably thinks we are all mental anyway. I don't know her very well, but from the last few days of getting to know her, she seems very confident, always laughing and has that beach bum vibe going on, lots of loose clothing, jean shorts, floaty dresses, sandals and sunglasses, she rocks it well. I wonder if she wears this in the winter though?

"It's complicated; there's this guy, and he's married," I confess.

"Tell me more..."

"Where do I even start?" I groan, so for the next half an hour, I fill them all in on the details of Taron and the mess I have gotten myself into, Sophie even nips down to get popcorn.

"Falling in love is hard," Trinity adds.

"What about you then, Trinity?" She looks a little put out by my question, but I am unsure why, seeing as she's just tried to grill me about the situation with Taron.

"No. There's no one."

"Bullshit," Cora replies. "Even at university, you never really got with anyone. It was always you, me and Adam. You are telling me from the sea of men that were there at university that no girl or boy took your fancy?"

"It just never really happened. We were always so busy working and studying," Trinity confesses. But her eyes are telling a different story. I don't know her that well either -maybe I am reading too much into this.

"How is the job search going?" Cora asks.

"A few months after your wedding, I am back out on tour, so I got the job!"

Cora squeals and throws her arms around Trinity, "That is amazing!"

"Yes, I have placed a spot with the travelling theatre, 'The Fairy Tale Christmas', so I will be up and down the country for all of December. I am so excited to be part of it. Gets me out of the city and seeing new places."

They go on about how she's playing the first violin and I lie back and close my eyes. I must have fallen asleep because when I woke up, I'm still fully clothed in Cora's bed, and this time, no dreaming.

Thankfully.

The wife - Taron

MUMFORD & SONS – LITTLE LION MAN

It has now been six weeks since my accident, incident, heart attack thingy, whatever you want to call this. The daily therapy is intense, the headaches even more so. And even though I remember scraps of moments here and there, post-traumatic amnesia headaches are awful. They can knock me out for hours. This is common, my doctor says. My doctor says a lot of things, I think mainly to reassure me (or the fact I pay him well), but I don't want reassurance. I want my memories back, all of them.

Four weeks of being here, in my home. But it doesn't feel like my home. It feels like I am on holiday, letting out someone else's house. This brain fog pisses me off. I would remember elements of my life, such as I knew my car was blue in my 20s, and that I had visited America with my parents when I was younger. But none of that crap is helping me right now. They're not strong memories linking me to this life I am in now.

Apparently, the doctor said it's normal to experience issues with memory for a few weeks after a concussion, and they are pleased with the fact that some memories are returning. Progress is measured in small steps or some shit like that. But what I also know is that they're becoming concerned that if the symptoms continue, then it is a sign of post-concussion syndrome (PCS). Because of this, I am starting a different treatment (or therapy) on Monday that'll help me recover from the memory loss of my mild traumatic brain injury, or whatever it is. Cognitive therapy has come highly recommended; the internet is raving about it and has an even bigger success rate. So, I am trying something else, something radical. I am doing what I can and whatever treatments are available to get my memories back. Thank goodness for my income because a lot of the treatments I have been trying have cost thousands of pounds, and if you can't pay upfront, it has a huge waiting list.

Being famous has its perks.

I have tried to journal my feelings. This, my therapist encourages, is a good way to manage memories and how I am feeling, but all I feel is frustration. I write everything down or put reminders on my phone in case I forget something. But it doesn't ease the fog in my head. It doesn't make me feel better.

I feel helpless. What a fucking feeling to have.

"Morning," I look up from my coffee and see my wife, Melissa, coming through to the open-plan kitchen. Her smile is forced. I can tell she is hurting, and I am sorry she is; I don't know how to rectify this situation. She pours a cup of coffee, her auburn hair is styled in a short wave, and she's wearing skinny jeans with a loose jumper. She looks lovely today. I'm still sleeping in the guest room. I haven't felt that connection with her yet, and sharing a bed with her feels wrong - a lie. I think we both thought that might change, but it hasn't. I knew that had upset her, but I didn't want to sleep in a bed with someone I didn't know. I am trying to be as honest as I can about everything, but that honesty just hurts Melissa, and I am at a loss.

We have continued to look at wedding photos, videos, holidays, past messages and still absolutely nothing. It's as if my brain has just shut down from her, a one-finger, fuck you.

Why doesn't my brain want to remember? Was our life so bad together? From what I gather, it wasn't. But how do I know the difference between a truth and a lie? What Melissa says, what my friends say, hell, even the internet reports, these could be totally different stories to how I actually felt.

I have tried so hard to be who I am meant to be, but I am still coming up with a blank. I lie awake most of the night, trying to remember. I am so damn frustrated. I hate being this stranger in my own home, in my own mind.

"How are you today?" I ask.

"Good, I thought we could take a walk today if you fancied?"

"Yes, I'd like that. I have a dinner meeting this evening with one of my sponsors. But it isn't until 7 pm."

"Do you want me to come with you?" I can see on her face that she doesn't want to come. In fact, for the last several days, Melissa has kept her distance. As if she is mentally pulling away from me, and there is not a damn thing I can do about that. I don't know how to comfort her or to know her better. She said that she hasn't been around much because she hasn't been feeling well, but I know it's because of me.

"No, it will be boring sponsor stuff, I think." She nods and helps to pack a bag of drinks and snacks, and then we head out to the car. After about half an hour, we arrive at a place called Morden Hall Park. The driver tells us he will be nearby if anything should arise. I should think that this is due to the entourage when we left the hospital. But Melissa was right; the hype has died down. But I think this is mainly down to me keeping a low profile. Apart from my daily walks in different parks around London and my treatments, I haven't really ventured from home socially. So, the media have termed me 'boring'.

We take a slow, quiet walk across the meadow and head along the Wandle trail. It is a quiet summer day and midweek, so there seem to be very few visitors around, which I am grateful for. The walk is calm and tranquil, easing the headache I have been nursing since I woke up. The river meanders alongside us, showcasing old water mills, the trees crisscross around, covering our path and giving us some privacy. And I like how at ease Melissa makes me feel, just like in the car. She seems to know me, to know us, and that brings me a small comfort. Even if Daisy still flits through my mind, a lot.

Seeing her at the park last week threw me off-centre, again. She was not like I had seen her before, dressed down, with no make-up, and hair all over the place, and she looked even more sexy than the last time I had seen her. All my feelings radiated to her, and I couldn't spare any of it for my own wife.

How fucked up is that?

Melissa slipped her hand into mine and I held it there. It feels nice, yet my brain still isn't catching up.

"What are we like as a couple?" The question surprises her as I haven't asked many about us. I really have tried to figure out this journey, this mess, on my own, but that doesn't seem to be working. Maybe this is my new strategy; maybe asking for help is the way forward to recovering my memories. She smiles warmly at me, nods over to a nearby bench and we sit facing one another.

"We fight a lot, but not in the way you think. More like we challenge each other, the Ying to my Yang. We have very different opinions, but we love that about each other. Such polar opposites, but we work as a team and love each other fiercely. You are loud but caring, opinionated, but respectful. You work hard, you're loyal, have the driest sense of humour, and always make me laugh." All those things she describes about me, she has this glint in her eye, yet I feel like now, I am none of those things.

Melissa leans forward and kisses me on the lips. It surprises me a little as she has not initiated any kind of contact, respecting my boundaries. I kiss her back with a softness, I place my hand on her warm cheek and relax into the kiss. She opens her mouth and slips her tongue into mine, I enjoy the sensation; I do the same, but then all I think about is the kiss with Daisy so I bring it quickly to an end. She looks at me expectantly and the glint in her eyes is replaced with sorrow.

"Did you feel or remember anything?" She already knows the answer as her eyes fill with tears and I shake my head slowly. I want to say yes, to be her everything, but still, I feel and remember absolute jack shit.

"Melissa," I stroke her tears away and cup her cheek again, "I am sorry. I want to love you the way you deserve. I want to be the person you want me to be. But I am not, I don't know how to be this person, your husband. I don't know what to do." She lets out a big sigh, takes my hand from her cheek and kisses the back of it.

"We will figure it out, Taron, we always do...come on, let's head back to the car."

I wish I had her optimism because each day, I feel we get further away from each other rather than closer together. That thought alone makes me feel very sad.

The night before - Daisy

TOM ODELL - HEAL

I wipe the sweat from my forehead as I run up the steps from the tube, taking two at a time. I know I am late, mega late, but this set of nights for work has been a killer. I don't know what is wrong with me; my brain has turned to Taron mush, and now I can't cope with night shifts, sleeping or anything. I seemed to be nodding off at any situation, hence my being late.

I took Kevin for a walk, not even a long one at that, and when I got back, I lay down on my bed. The next minute, two hours passed and now I am running bloody late. I weave in and out of the early evening people, mostly tourists. Being in the centre of London is a pain up the bum, so many people descended to London during the late summer. And, of course, Cora wanted somewhere central for her pre-wedding dinner. Easy for me to get to and easy for Cole to get to as well. It's just not so easy now, as I can't seem to walk faster than a snail's pace with everyone stopping to look at all the different shops and the street entertainment.

My phone buzzes, but I reject the call. I know it's Cora, wanting to have a go at me for being late, I am nearly there, so she can wait as I would prefer only to be moaned at once. I push the damp hair off my face and I'm so happy when I enter the air-conditioned Italian restaurant, wishing I could loiter in the doorway just to cool down for a few moments. I scan the restaurant floor and see that they are sitting towards the back. I approach the table and Cora rolls her eyes. Cole stands and en-velopes me in a hug, giving me a kiss on the cheek as he pulls back.

"Daisy, you look well," I smile.

"You too, Cole. Did you lose weight?" I am surprised at how much weight he has lost. He looks good and healthier, and his hair has now disappeared. But he suited the bald look, even if his dark hair was still trying to poke through. He'd grown a moustache and it made me miss Dad's, which is ridiculous.

What an odd thing to think.

But whenever Cole is around, I think a lot of Dad. I hadn't seen Cole in a few years, but he was the kind of person that no matter when you had been in his company, you picked right back up where you left off. Cole is amazing, Dad could not have picked a better boyfriend. He stuck around when he didn't have to; he became my legal guardian and picked me up off the floor when I was so low. In my teenage years, I held onto a lot of guilt and regret from Dad dying. When Dad had his heart attack, I was only in the next room. I was too busy shoving my fake lashes and tan on even to take note of what was going on around me. I often wondered what would have happened if I had got up earlier or, if I hadn't been so self-absorbed with how I looked at school just to fit in. Had he cried out and I hadn't heard him? Had he shouted for me in his last moments? If I had noticed and ran into his room just a few minutes earlier and carried out CPR, would he still be alive now?

It had circled around my head for months before I spoke to Cole about it. I was hurting so bad that I felt I was drowning in my own guilt. Cora had disappeared (ran away) back to university, dealing with her own shit. But I felt that she had left me too. But in reality, we all didn't know how to cope or be there for one another. I really struggled. But Cole was patient; he sat and listened to me when I needed it most. The amount of love I had for Cole was endless, He had carried my sadness and our burden as well when he could have left me, too. But he didn't. How do you move on from a loved one dying?

You don't.

"You're late," Cora snarks, giving me the sister's death eyes. I shuffle over and hug her anyway. I know she is in a bad mood, but I can't help that I love a good nap. It's my happy place, napping, drinking, dog walks, pudding (obviously) and Pringles – once you open a tube of them, they're gone. I can't even blame Kevin, as he doesn't eat human food - and sex is up there in the top ten, too. But with the amount of sexual tension radiating from my body with Taron, that seems to be my not-so-happy place at the moment.

It is official that Taron had ruined me - emotionally and sexually.

"I fell asleep. The nights at the hospital have caught up with me. I'm sorry," even though she still looked pissed, she didn't mention it again.

"How is it going in the hospital? Are you still loving it?"

I miss Cole's warmth, the father figure I needed in my life after Dad died and even now. I know that Dad and Cole loved each other so much – I often wondered if they would have gotten married. During the months that Cole lived with us, I have never seen Dad so happy, they loved fiercely and we all laughed so much. We were a family. Then Dad died. So now I have tasked myself with a lifetime of saving as many people as I can to make up for my failure.

"Yes, I love it. I wouldn't be anywhere else. I just wish I wasn't so bloody tired."

"Well, you better be on your 'A' game tomorrow, Daisy. If you dare fall asleep, you will feel my wrath," my sister jokes.

"Oh, I wonder why? What is happening tomorrow, I wonder?" I smirk back at her. Cole fills my glass with Prosecco and raises his glass. We both follow suit.

"To you, Cora. Thank you for asking me to walk you down the aisle tomorrow. I'm honoured that you asked, and I am so proud of you...I know your Dad would be, too," his voice hitches at the end. I look at Cora and see that tears are already forming in her eyes, and mine are glassy as well.

Would he be proud of me, too?

Cora chokes back a sob, and that's it; we are all letting go of our tears, both happy and sad.

"See, this is why we should see you more, Cole. We are in each other's company for only a few moments and we are all in tears," Cora moans.

Cole smiles at us both. I have truly missed him. After Dad died, he stayed in England until I was 18 and finished my A-Levels. He ensured I was okay and taken care of. He didn't want to burden Cora, he didn't want Cora to come back and take care of me, or, I go to her and uproot my life. For that, I would forever be grateful.

"Well," he wipes away his tears, "your Dad was the most amazing person I have ever met. He changed my life; you all did. I know I live out in Hong Kong now, but it doesn't mean I love you guys any less, I will always be here for you. Both of you." He grabs both of our hands in turn.

Dad would have totally married him.

We each order a pizza and catch up. It's a great night and I'm sad when it ends. He pays for everything despite our protests. Cole makes the remark about how he loves treating his girls.

What an amazing man Cole is.

The wedding morning –
Daisy

BRUNO MARS – MARRY YOU

"Are you nervous?" I ask Cora as we lie, snuggled under the blankets together in the hotel bed. It's nice just to have this calm moment together before her wedding day. To be honest, the last time we snuggled like this was when Dad died. I remember crawling into her bed like a small child and sobbing in her arms. Losing Dad at sixteen was one of the worst experiences of my life. Losing a parent is like losing a part of yourself that you will never find or get back. It is that unconditional love that no matter what you say or do, they always love you, and that was ripped from me at such a young age and shattered my heart. It isn't something a person ever gets over. I just realised that I got better at hiding it. After a while, people stopped asking how I was or giving me that sympathetic look. I guess people forget and carry on with their lives. When I met new people at university, they didn't know my past, any of it. But it is always there, an invisible pain, a scar across my heart. It's the little silly things I miss, really, like when I passed my 3 A levels and I wanted to ring him and share the news. Or when I saw something funny, I wanted to tell Dad; he had the driest sense of humour, the most memorable laugh and an excellent Donald Duck impression. It's the little silly things I miss.

"No...yes...maybe a little," she confesses and smiles. I look at my watch, it's a little after 8 am, and the wedding isn't until 4 pm, but neither of us could sleep much. Cora was excited and irritable all night, and I, I have an excitable and irritable Taron problem. He lives under my skin. He set fire to my bruised heart as if his soul called to mine. It is ridiculous how his body makes me feel when he is near. I stare at my sister as we are both lost in thought.

"Dad would be so proud of you," I whisper. Her eyes immediately become glossy, and a tear escapes her eye.

"Cole, last night, now you, it's like you want me to be tearful," she chuckles.

"Maybe not the 'fucking the teacher' part," we giggle, "but he would be. I mean, look how happy you are; look how far you've come in your career. The London Orchestra was just a pipe dream for you growing up and you made it real. You did that," she chuckles.

"Do you really think he would be proud of us? I really miss him more today," I pull my sister closer and hold her in my arms. I feel her silent tears drip into my neck.

"Me too. I miss him so much. He has missed everything..." I have found, over the years, that grief isn't the loss of just a person. It's the loss of the thousands of tiny things you don't get to share or experience with them anymore. Like today, with Cora. He would be gutted to have missed this. My thoughts turn to Mum. "Did you ever think of inviting Mum?"

"Fuck no," she pulls away and looks at me, wiping away her tears, concern, etches her face, "do you think I should have?"

"Fuck no!" We giggle, and she lies on her back, staring at the ceiling. "She doesn't deserve you. She doesn't deserve us!"

"Where do you think she is right now?" I sigh.

"Cora, I love you as a sister, but you can't do that to yourself. She is selfish and only cares about herself and her next hit. Yes, she will always be our mum, and I know you remember a lot more of the good times than me. But my memories of her growing up are of her shouting, being cruel and passing out on the sofa from too much drink, telling me I am worthless and then repeatedly leaving us...thank goodness we had such a great Dad." Cora turns on her side and strokes my hair, looking at me with a tinge of sadness.

"You are not worthless, you know that, right?" I smile at my sister. It took a long time to get over that comment. I never told Dad about it as I knew it would have broken his heart if he had heard half the stuff Mum had said to us. I think he would have been broken just as much as us. She was sly like that.

I thought back to the last time I saw Mum, over five years ago. It was over a year since Dad had passed away; things were semi-normal, I guess.

I turned 18 and got the predicted grades I needed to get into university. But that Spring was weird because Mum showed up as if nothing had happened. She had been released from prison many months before and conveniently came looking for us just as we were putting the house up for sale. She played the victim of how heartbroken she was. Poor Cole didn't know what to do with himself. Mum was around every day crying, saying how much she loved Dad and how she didn't know that he had died (even though Cora had written to her, I don't know why she bothered). Her alcoholic breath reeked the house out and she smelt like yesterday's nightclub. Jail had been unkind to her and she looked a lot older than in her 50s.

She made a good show of it every day for months. To be honest, despite her drinking, I did start to believe that she was genuinely upset. I think what got me was that she really did try with me. She took a genuine interest in my studies and even helped me revise for my exams. Her promises were a bit hit-and-miss, but you could tell she was making a genuine effort – because at that time we didn't realise her motivation.

A great actress, that's what she was; maybe this was how she fooled Dad for so long. Despite her kindness, I still felt hurt that she'd missed so much that I tried to keep her at arm's length. Being a cynic, I often asked why she was so interested in our lives all of a sudden. Even Cora was happily surprised, stating that prison had changed her for the better and that maybe this was her making amends. But if she wanted to make amends, why did it take over seven months from her being released from prison to come and see us?

When my exams had finished, I decided it was time to make my move to London and the house went up for sale. Cole had secured a job overseas in Hong Kong as a teacher. He debated if it was a good choice to leave me, but I told him it was time and gave that friendly push. He had done more than enough. He really did want to go back to Dubai, but after his sudden departure to be with Dad, there were a lot of rumours spread at that school of him being gay. He knew he would not be welcome back – seeing as it is illegal in that country. He also didn't want to risk it again, even though he said Dad was worth the risk. Cole said he needed a new and exciting country to explore and settled on going to Hong Kong. I wanted to tell him to stay because I would miss him as he had been amazing, but I knew I had to grow up and move on, too.

Then Mum pulled out the big guns. One morning, after a few days of Mum being AWOL, we received a letter from a solicitor. It detailed that Mum wanted and was entitled to half of the money when the sale was finalised.

So, there it was in black and white, what she really wanted. Not her daughters or grieving her ex-husband. She wanted the money. Cora was distraught and it really rocked her. Cole was in utter shock and disbelief. Call me a cynical bugger, but my gut never lies and I felt it deep down inside that something didn't feel right. Nevertheless, it hurt like a bitch because, after all, she was still our mum. Right there and then, my walls came back up, that loving her was a pile of shit; she didn't deserve to know Cora or me properly. Cole wanted to fight it. He said it wasn't right and that she was cheating us out of our future and our inheritance. I, on the other hand, wanted out. I made a call to the solicitor (probably the most grown-up thing I had ever done at the time) and accepted the agreement on the premise that if she had half the house equity, she also agreed she would never ask for money or come near us again. She agreed almost instantly, even though part of me hoped she would say no, and guess what? We have never seen her since.

The knock on the door pulls me from my thoughts. I begrudgingly get out of bed, I open the door to see Trinity, Sophie and the hair and make-up lady outside the room.

"Let's get this mother fucking day started," screeched Trinity. I laugh and let them in. The morning is an awesome experience of bucks fizz and mocktails, lots of laughing, and nibbling on the delicious hotel room service. We all went for similar make-up, the smokey eye, to go with our beautiful red dresses, all in different styles. I had a plunge-long dress, Trinity had a spaghetti-strap red dress that shimmered and Sophie went with an off-the-shoulder look. My hair is pulled up into a sophisticated side ponytail with twists and whisps of curly hair. Thank goodness I had time to grow it a little longer for this style. I top it off with deep red lipstick and red shoes to match. I look in the mirror inwardly praising my Spanx. I look thinner and whatever contouring that makeup woman had done to my face, jeez, I need to take a lot of photos of myself today to remember this moment. I feel and look amazing.

"I'd bang you," Trinity quirks as she stands behind me in the mirror, "you look hot!"

I laugh and turn to look her over, too, blowing out a low whistle, "So do you." There's another knock on the door. Amy, Zach's daughter and Hope, Sophie's daughter, are ushered in, whilst Oliver, Sophie's boyfriend, hides his eyes under his hands.

"I am not looking, ladies, I promise," his smooth Scottish accent calls out to the room. I try not to dribble a little at him because he is a beautiful man. When he was on the television show "Always Famous," I used to watch and think him, Toby, and Luke could all be my fake boyfriends. They were walking models who could sing, dance, act and be in my imagination any time of the day or night. I laugh to myself and shake away the teenage thought. Sophie met him when she moved up north, near Scotland, and their friendship blossomed into love.

"You can look, Oliver. It's fine," Sophie laughs.

"Mamma," Hope runs into the room and hugs Sophie, "You look beautiful," I watch as Oliver takes his hands from his eyes, his face is a picture. His mouth drops to the floor, and something wicked pools in his eyes. Sophie does look amazing, although she has a strapless red dress on to match us; her hair is black underneath and a deep red on top, all curled and her make-up is flawless. I always thought she was a beautiful person growing up, and as a teenager, I tried to copy her outfits and make-up styles. She smiles shyly back as she puts Hope down.

"Holy shit, you look incredible!" Oliver beams. I love the way he looks at her, the way Zach looks at my sister. I want someone to walk into a room and look at me like that, that I am the only person in that room. Does Taron look at me like that?

"What does shit mean?" Hope asks - a great question asked by a five-year-old.

"I said ship, Hope, ship," Oliver retorts. We all laugh, but Sophie tuts. He crosses the room in two strides and kisses Sophie with such lust and desire that I look away, embarrassed for them. A little pang of jealousy hits me in the heart.

I want that. I really do. I never have before, but I am starting to want that. I feel that I am changing, wanting different things in my life, like love.

"Ewwww, get a room," Amy whines. She's in a three-quarter-length dress, her hair is in soft waves and she has a lot of make-up on, so I know that Cora will be a bit annoyed. But it is for a special occasion, I am sure it is fine for one day. Amy immediately takes her phone out and plonks herself on the chair in the corner of the room.

She's such a social creature, not!

"I would get a room if you all get out," Oliver jokes as he pulls away from Sophie, both of them breathless. He walks back towards the door, "That's a warm-up for later," he remarks as he closes the door with the biggest wink and dirty grin on his face. I laugh. Even I am a little turned on by that possessive display.

Hope, Sophie's daughter, comes over to me and twirls in her bridesmaid's dress and starts throwing petals at me, laughing.

At least I know she's practised.

"Good job, I brought a few bags of them, but remember you throw them on the ground when we walk down the aisle," I laugh and give her a little tickle. She giggles and I see a glimmer of Stefan in her. I hate it when I see him, and it always makes me sad. Pushing that horrible thought to one side, as I am not going to do this in my head today. Today is all about Cora. I walk over and knock on the bedroom door.

"All okay?" I ask.

"Yep, nearly done, don't come in. I want it to be a surprise," Cora calls back. When she emerges from the door a few moments later, we all gasp; there is not a dry eye in sight, well, apart from Amy and Hope – but they don't count. She looks absolutely perfect. I am so proud of her, so proud to be her sister.

Her dress is an open back, white lace with a line of sweetheart straps and a chapel train, so much lace and so perfect. It makes her boobs look full and her body curvy. Her hair is styled up with twists and beautiful, delicate, diamanté butterfly clips have been inserted into her hair. She is wearing the diamond necklace that Dad gave to her for her sixteenth birthday.

"Okay, no more crying, or you will ruin my makeup, and then I will have to kill you all!" Cora declares.

At about 3 p.m., the photographer turns up with Cole in tow. He looks so smart, dressed in a suit. He is the best stand-in for Dad. The fact that he is here, that he wants to be here for us both, makes him such an amazing person. We weren't even family by blood, but he is the best non-Dad I have ever had.

Cole burst into tears at the sight of Cora, which had us all crying again. "Cora, if your dad were here for this, my goodness, he would be speech-less," Cole gushed.

It is time to get my sister married.

The wedding afternoon - Daisy

BEYONCE - HALO

Cole, Cora, Amy, Hope, Trinity and I stand outside the oldest music hall in London. Something both Cora and Zach had a strong connection with. Music brought them together, so the music would solidify their marriage together; it is very romantic. Even though everyone else is now inside, there are only 11 of us here (well, 13 if you count the registrar and her assistant). The wedding party is small, but they have hired out the whole place exclusively; it's fricking awesome. As I enter the building, I am in awe of the interior, with the Victorian staircase and the old, deep-painted wooden floors giving it that extra oldy-worldy feel; it looks so special. There are fairy lights hung from the ceiling, brightly shining in the dimly lit room, which criss-crosses all around the edges of the twisted columns and the balcony, too. It looks so magical that it takes my breath away.

As Hope and I walk down the aisle, I look at the little miracle; she is throwing petals everywhere, and it is too cute. I laugh and then focus on the music playing; it's *The Piano* by Aidan Gibbons, another memory that Cora says brought them together. I love how all of this is so personal to them. I have been to a couple of weddings over the last few years, and they were big and loud and a little over the top, but if that is how you want to get married, I am all for it. But my sister's wedding feels different. It feels intimate and beautiful and a wash of contrasting sadness consumes me. It's of a longing for something I never knew I wanted.

Until right now.

We walk towards the stage at the front of the auditorium, which has a huge Z and C brightly lit letters and the edge of the stage is filled with wildflowers, ones that are very similar to what Zach turned up with to profess his love to Cora after her first show. It was the same first show that she refused me and Cole to come to. I am so in love with the beauty of the architecture as there is so much musical history and character that I truly understood why they wanted to be married here.

It is perfect for them.

The room isn't large, but it is odd that there are only a few chairs for the service. Even though this is perfect for Cora, it still made me sad that she didn't want to invite more people, to fill the room with joy, to bear witness to their love. We make it to the top of the aisle without any mishaps. Sophie is all smiles and a look of relief. I smile over at Zach and Oliver, the best man, and then I watch as Amy and Trinity come up the aisle looking perfect and full of smiles. I think this is the biggest smile I have seen on Amy; it suits her, and she should do it more often. Her Dad, Zach, has the proudest look on his face; their relationship as father and daughter is so lovely. He raised her practically himself, and he did such a fabulous job. I nod at Zach's Aunt Sheila, who gives me a small wave back. She has a tissue clasped in her hand; she looks like she has done her fair share of crying already. I smile at Adam, Cora's friend from university, but he seems in a daze; he has the biggest frown on his face; maybe he's unwell.

Cora enters the room with Cole and I try so hard not to cry, but it's too late. She is a picture of perfection. I sneak a look at Zach and see his face; it's like his dreams have come true all at once. Now he is crying, too. He looks back to the front and then the ceiling for a moment as if he can't contain his excitement. Zach then looks at Cora again wiping away the tears, the look morphs into relief, pride, and then hunger. I had seen that similar hunger face on Taron when we kissed.

Crap, I'm thinking of him again!

Cole, lets go of Cora. "You hurt her, I will cut off your balls," we all laugh, "Just because I haven't said it yet, Zach, doesn't mean it's not true." He gives Zach a handshake and kisses Cora on the cheek, and stands beside me, Amy and Trinity. Hope has wandered off to sit with Sophie.

The registrar greets and starts the ceremony. Zach is holding Cora's hand and is all smiles; he doesn't even look nervous; he looks so happy. They exchange vows, which I am excited to hear as they have been super secretive about it.

"Cora," his voice is shaking, maybe a little nervous then, he clears his throat. "When I first met you in the bar that winter's day, I could not believe my luck; I thought you were beautiful, funny and we had so much in common; I still do think these things, by the way," he smirks and Cora smiles. "Honestly, I think I fell in love with you right there and then. I mean, what came after was a little trickier," she smiles wider, and we all giggle, "but I couldn't ignore my heart and my feelings for you. I promise to be there for you no matter what, I love the way you loved me and Amy, from the get-go. I promise to love you no matter what because without you, life doesn't exist properly." He slides the wedding band onto her finger and swipes another tear from his face. She cups his cheek for a moment, gazing deep into his eyes. The registrar clears her throat and Cora smiles sheepishly.

"Zach, you consumed all of my thoughts when we met and still do, to be honest. You were there for me when I was at my lowest, patient, kind, caring and not once did you make me feel I was less of a person. You've done everything to support me, push me to be a better person and welcomed me into your family with Amy, who I promise to love just as much as you. Thank you for being my person, my one, and I promise to love you until my last breath." She slides on his wedding band, and they hold one another's hands.

"I now pronounce you man and wife. Mr and Mrs Jones, everyone," the registrar exclaims. We all cheer and holler, and the wedding couple kiss.

Once the ceremony is over, the pictures are taken. My cheeks hurt from all the smiling I have had to do; I dread to think how Cora feels. They are off in the other part of the hall, having the last of their wedding pictures taken. We are served a few nibbles and a glass of bubbly whilst we wait for them to finish and head to the reception. I notice that Trinity has that dreamy look in her eyes, and when I follow her line of vision, it's on Adam.

"I see the way you look at him, Trinity." She looks surprised for a moment, then sadness washes her face.

"I love him," she whispers.

"Wow!" After the talk at the hen party, when she admitted to liking nobody and then suddenly a confession, something doesn't add up.

"I've loved him for years," she adds.

"Okay, so why aren't you telling him this?" I ask.

"Just look and you will see," I stare at Adam for a few moments; he looks smart in his suit. I can appreciate that he is quite good-looking, and the wearing glasses vibe has got it going for him. I like the shaggy blonde hair on him, too. He definitely needed to be in a punk band or something. I look back at Trinity, confused.

"I don't get it," I admit.

"Can't you see the way he looks at Cora?" I look back and he practically lights up every time she is near. He was in love with her. Did Cora know this?

"Shit," she nods. I notice the glassy look in her eyes.

"I can't compete with that. He doesn't look at me the way he looks at her."

"I am so sorry, that's...shit."

"Yeah, I know. We don't see each other very often, so I guess I am only reminded when we are all together. But every time I have tried to get into a relationship, I just want Adam, and he doesn't even see me. He has friend zoned me so far in that I am never getting out and he only ever saw her. I think he will only ever see her." I hug her close for a moment.

"Why don't you show him?"

"I have thought about it...a lot. But I don't want to be second best, I want to be someone's everything, you know?"

I didn't know, but with Taron, I was starting to understand the importance of being someone, being needed and wanted.

The wedding night – Daisy

THE WEEKND – CALL OUT MY NAME

My sister and now my new brother-in-law, Zach (Mr and Mrs Jones), have hired a semi-private room at the glorious hotel that is The Ritz in Mayfair. The room they have hired usually only accommodates eight people, but I convinced them that because of the special occasion (and some of the guests were children), we would happily squeeze in. They are very friendly and accommodating, thankfully. The room has a Louis XVI ambience. With its thick draped curtains and floor-to-ceiling mirrors, it is perfect. I love the marble columns.

The Michelin-style dinner is beautiful and intimate, I can eat here forever and be a happy, well-fed lady. The chatter at the table is easy and relaxed and everyone seems happy and well fed. During one of the courses, I gave Cora and Zach their wedding present. When she opens the card, she lets out a little shrill scream. Cole and I have booked one of the suites upstairs for Cora and Zach. I had a little look at it earlier and nearly vomited. It is something straight out of a film, with a spacious bedroom and dining room. I am sure that the sheets cost more than my monthly rent, and the antique furniture is unbelievable. If Dad was here, he would have missed the wedding and fanboyed all over the artistic setup.

I am now packed to the brim with delicious food that I will probably have dreams about for months to come, I am ready to explode. I am now hating this bridesmaid dress with a passion. I could barely breathe in it before I ate all of the food, and now my Spanx is digging into some ungodly places. As we make our way over to The Rivoli bar, I try to rearrange myself in the most ladylike manner.

Nope, it did not happen. This place is far too upmarket for my liking. Everyone is staring at me like I am an alien as I pull my Spanx up and out of all of the folds of my bum.

At around 9 p.m., Oliver takes Hope and Amy back to the Premier Inn with Zach's Aunt Sheila. It is only a tube stop across to Leicester Square, but they decide to take an Uber for ease. Hope is already fast off, and Amy is moaning that at almost 15 years old, she should be able to stay up longer, but I think Zach and Cora want some alone time, and I can't blame them.

After they leave, I settle in and drink my cocktail whilst everyone is chatting and marvel at The Rivoli bar, as it is breathtaking. The golden trim makes it look like it's real; it oozes lavishness with its wood-panelled walls. When I sit on one of their plush seats, I decide I want to live here; my bum feels like it's on holiday. Their cocktails are amazing, fruity and delicious. The bartender has impeccable service. He seems to know exactly what I want to drink when I say that I am unsure and want something light and fruity.

I love getting something that I didn't even know I wanted; it makes it even more delicious.

About an hour after that, Adam decides to make a swift exit. He says that he has an early start tomorrow, but I see it written all over his face now that he's suffering. I don't know what he expected from my sister. Did he want her to stop the wedding and declare her love for him? It's clear that she is head over heels in love with Zach, but, after they said I do, his posture and face got lower with each hour that passed. I think it has finally sunk in, that she doesn't feel the same way. I know a good few years back, they had a little thing after my Dad died, but he seems to be burning his candle bright for her for years. But she blew it off as soon as Zach came back on the scene—a harsh reality. I really had no idea, I just thought they were really good friends. He says goodbye to everyone and leaves. I make an excuse to go to the toilet, noticing Trinity has a similar look on her face to Adam.

The defeated look.

I catch up with Adam in the hotel's circular lobby, which opens up to all floors. I feel that I am not in the centre of London, but on holiday in some beautiful Italian architectural spectacular. Its floors are covered with a 1980s thick plush carpet and everything shouts regal, posh and quaint. With its open circular levels, long chandeliers and draperies, I honestly feel like I am on the Titanic with all its beautiful designs – throw in a young Leo DiCaprio and I am set!

I love it here!

"Adam!" I call out, but he doesn't turn. I semi-jog towards him, which is always a bad idea for me, especially in this dress. It may have disastrous consequences if I am not careful. I pull him back gently by his shoulders.

"What, Daisy!?" He turns to face me, looking mad, but as I step closer, there are tears in his eyes. My face falls, and I realise that he is hurting badly. Always one for cuddles, I pull him into the biggest bear hug.

"Oh, Adam," I whisper as he silently shakes with a sob, "I'm sorry," we hold one another for a few moments, and it is so odd to have such an intimate moment with, I guess, a stranger. He pulls away and backhands his tears.

"I have to go," he mumbles as he stares at the floor, "I can't stay…" he looks at me as he turns to leave, "Please don't mention this to Cora." He doesn't wait for my answer, I watch for a moment as he disappears out the lobby door.

Love stinks!

It makes me so sad that he is hurting. I honestly don't think Cora has any idea how he feels about her. I walk along the long gallery, inhaling all the different fresh flower scents and head to the toilet to reapply some makeup. My hair still looks amazing; my make-up only needed a little top-up. To say that I have been like this for the last 7 hours, I am still rocking this outfit, makeup and hairstyle. I take a quick selfie and send it to the university girls' chat so that I can document that I scrub up well, for once. I wander back towards the bar and bump into a steel wall. I look up, ready to apologise but stop.

Taron.

Honestly, does he have a tracker on me or something?

"Daisy," he nods his head and jeez, he's in jeans and a tight t-shirt. Is there anything that this man can't wear that doesn't make him look like a Greek god?

"Why do we keep meeting? Are you following me?" He laughs a deep and sexy rumble.

"I had a meeting with one of my sponsors. I was just heading home..." he looks at me from head to toe, and oh my shit, I think I nearly orgasm on the spot with the way he is undressing me with his eyes, "You look incredible," he finally breathed.

"It's my sister's wedding...have you been drinking?" Such a stupid thing to say, but the way he openly looks at me with such desire has me on edge.

He arches an eyebrow at me, "No, have you?"

"Of course...." I want to ask him to stay, but I know it's a bad idea. Before my brain catches up, I ask anyway. "Would you like to stay for a drink?"

"I would like that very much, Daisy," he smiles, and I think I have gone to mouth and vagina heaven.

Stop it, Daisy!

We walk back into the Rivoli bar and it feels like I am bringing my first boyfriend home, unsure how they would all react and oddly nervous. Zach notices first with the biggest smile on his face when he recognises who I am with.

"Everyone, this is Taron," everyone looks up and is horribly silent. Zach stands first and shakes his hand.

"A pleasure to meet you, Taron, a big fan," he adds. Taron smiles with such confidence that it's ridiculous. Why is he not as nervous as I am?

"Holy shit, you are more beautiful in real life," Trinity hollers; she looks around, not even embarrassed by her outburst. "I think that is my cue to leave. Come on, Sophie, you sexy lady, let's Uber out of this joint." They hug everyone goodbye; I notice Trinity holds onto Taron a little longer and whispers, "You smell incredible."

"Right, I am off too, girls, " Cole admits, although he seems a bit upset, or is he uncomfortable? He's got that frown between his eyes that he gets when he's thinking or seeing something he doesn't like.

I hope it's not Taron being here.

Cole and I hug, making quick plans to pick him up in a few days and take him to the airport. Then, there were only four of us left. Taron orders lemon water and smiles warmly at Cora and Zach.

"We are going to head to bed, too," Cora adds. Zach's face falls as I think he wants to grill Taron about everything football. I know Zach supports Taron's team, but then we all know what he is going upstairs for, so his smile is then replaced with desire as he smacks Cora's bum.

"Come, Mrs Jones, let me take you to bed," he takes her by the hand and kisses the back of it. "I love calling you that wifey," he coos.

"I don't think I will tire of hearing you say that, husband," she purrs back as he leads her away. She gives me a cheeky smile and wink.

Everyone leaving is subtle, not! I don't know if I can be alone with him.

However, the conversation is easy; we talk for hours, drinking and laughing. He is perfect and is someone I could easily fall in love with, which scares the crap out of me. I have never entertained that thought, but knowing this now, I have to keep my feelings in check.

He is married, Daisy, don't do it!

But I want to, I want to so bad I feel it bubbling inside me. The urge to rip off his clothes, ride his dick and touch his manly chest hair all night long is one fantasy I want to become a reality.

The bar is about to close, and the staff are tidying around us, so we reluctantly leave. I'm feeling a little jittery about us, either parting ways or not, but I need the toilet to take a minute. I excuse myself and make my way down to the toilets to freshen up. I lean against the sink and take a deep breath. I hear the door go, and it's Taron. I look up in surprise and turn to him.

"Is everything okay?" I ask, confused by the fact that he has come into the ladies' room.

"Yes," he says breathlessly as he stalks towards me with a wildness in his eyes and then all of a sudden, his perfect lips are on mine. He pulls me close and it takes my breath away. His tongue is in my mouth, and I can't stop it. I know it shouldn't be happening, but I want this. I want all of him; we groan into one another's mouths, and my hands are in his curly, soft hair, and his manly pine scent is intoxicating. I angle my head to the side so that I can deepen my tongue into his warm mouth and he is attacking mine in the most beautiful way. I am so turned on. If he slammed me against the wall, pulled out his dick and fucked me, I wouldn't say no; I want him.

He is married, Daisy!

I push him away, seeing a glimmer of reason.

"What are you doing?" I demand, "What are we doing? Why did we just do that?"

"You know why, you feel this too." Every time our eyes meet, it scrambles my brain. "I seem to do a lot of things with you that, apparently, I don't normally do. People keep telling me I am different, that I am not the same, but what happens if this is me now? What if we were meant to be together, that we were meant to meet?"

"It's the Nightingale effect or syndrome," I confess.

"The what?" he asks confused.

"I saved your life, and now you feel like you owe me. The person feels love and affection towards the patient or the caregiver."

He studies me for a moment. "Is that how you feel about me?"

I walked into that one. "Yes and no. I lost my dad at a young age," I admit.

"Oh, I'm sorry."

"Thanks, but you don't need to be. He died from a heart attack," I'm not sure why I am telling him this so openly, without emotion; I never do this. Admitting to Dad's death always makes me feel uncomfortable, but I need Taron to understand that this can't happen; this is not real, no matter how we feel.

"Oh," I study his face as he realises what I have said, and then a look of sadness shadows it.

"I couldn't save him," I whisper, hoping that the tears will not make an appearance.

"But you saved me," he adds.

"I saved you," he thinks for a long hard moment.

"And you think this is the reason why we have feelings for one another?"

I have to say it, he is married and it has to end no matter how much I want him inside me or how desperate I am to touch him. He is married. I wasn't going to be the person to break this marriage up. "Yes," I whisper, not wanting to meet his intense, alluring stare.

"Okay." He responds.

What? Did he agree just like that?

I look back into his deep, pooling eyes. He looks angry. "I am going to go." I feel sadness radiate through my body. I didn't want him to leave, not really. "Can I say a few things before I do?" I nod, desperate to be in his company before he leaves my life forever. "Firstly, Daisy, you are a terrible liar. Secondly, I think the Nightingale speech is a big load of shit because you're scared of what this might be; guess what? Me too. And thirdly, married or not, people can't help who they fall in and out of love with. It's what makes life so exciting. I feel all of this for you, Daisy, for you; I can't stop thinking about you. Yes, I might not know who I am exactly at the moment, but I know how I feel and what I want...I want you, Daisy."

We stare at each other for a few moments, our breathing laboured, but no matter what he says, I cannot be with another man who is married. I think he might kiss me again and temptation is a bitch because I want him to devour me, but he turns abruptly and leaves.

"Goodbye," I whisper to no one, feeling an overwhelming wave of tiredness and sadness consume my body.

Paparazzi suck - Daisy

RHANNA – SHUT UP AND DRIVE

I stood in the ladies' toilets at the Ritz for several moments and then I did the oddest thing. I cried. Why am I so invested in this non-relationship? Why is he making me feel things that I swore when Dad died, I would not feel again? I did not want to be left feeling so vulnerable again, yet Taron, the utter shit monster, seems to be around me in five seconds and I am like Kevin on heat or a teenager with love hearts in her eyes. He is pulling all sorts of emotions out of me that I thought were dead and buried, especially after what happened with Stefan.

What is wrong with you, Daisy? Is this early menopause, or am I mentally regressing with too many hormones?

I got a taxi home; I don't care that it cost £46. I am not riding the tube in this state. I felt really alone and sad and I haven't felt like this in years. When I arrive home, I don't bother to take off the makeup or the dress, even if it is slightly suffocating me. I let Kevin out for a quick wee and then I hide under my quilt, letting the last few hours float around my head. I think I finally fell asleep around 4 am in the morning. I was so happy to be at home, in my own bed, because being anywhere else other than my bed would have made me feel even worse. I always feel like I can't sleep well unless it's in my own bed and I need to sleep, compress and internalise.

He kissed me, and then he left. Taron kissed me again. I can't deny it was the hottest and the best kiss I had ever had, and I have kissed some fantastic people in my life as well. Maybe because I feel invested in Taron, with the whole drama that surrounds it all that makes it even more exciting.

Or maybe it is because I saved him, and it's the nightingale effect.

But I am not a bitch and I feel proud of myself that I stopped the kiss. I didn't want to stop it, I wanted him to fuck me so bad. I wanted him to kiss me all over and moan out his name, then for him to lift me up onto the vanity in that bathroom, pull my dress up slowly whilst I ran my hands through his dark, curly hair and...

He is married. Stop these dirty thoughts!

What crap is all this? I roll over from my dream rant and hear my phone buzzing. It's a little after 8 a.m. and I hate this! Why, for the love of all things related to my sleep-god, will you not let me have a peaceful sleep or lie in? I drank far too much last night and got turned on far too much. I have all this energy; I need to scream out loud or sleep it off but all I get is the rude awakening of...Cora. I want to throw my phone across the room that she is calling me this early.

"What, Cora?" I answer with a shitty attitude, "Surely, you should be sucking dick, or at least have vagina pain exhaustion from all that sex last night, that you don't need to ring me at 8 am!"

"Oh my god, Daisy, that's disgusting! What did you do last night?"

"Why?" I turn on my camera so we can video call. I am face down in the bed knowing full well I have dribble and a nest of hair. My bed is my happy place.

"You look like shit. Did you not even get undressed?" My sister laughs, just because she's had time to shower and is gifted in the 'how great I can look in 5 minutes' department.

Fuck off!

"Why Cora?" I snap. I feel my phone buzz.

"Check your phone. Man, I get married and this shite happens. You can't give me one night of it all being about me," she is pouting when I open my eyes to look at what she has sent me.

I open the message and click the link sent. There in black and white, or in this case colour, is mine and Taron's picture from last night in the bar. We are huddled very close together and it looks like we are kissing. The headline reads, 'Premier footballer has lost his mind and cheats!'

My stomach drops, "Shit!" I bolt up out of bed.

"Shit indeed," Cora agrees, "what the hell happened?" she demands.

"Well, it's obvious we kissed," I respond sarcastically, "not in this picture, we aren't...we kissed in the bathroom."

"Well, I was still gonna ask if you did. I know how the press can be a bit crap and warp things." I know she is referring to Sophie and all the shit she got in the press when she became pregnant because of Stefan's (AKA the dickhead) actions.

"Nope, it definitely happened." We sigh collectively.

"Was he as good as we hoped?" she smirks.

I groan, "Not helping."

"What are you going to do?"

"Nothing, I am going to do nothing!" I cry.

"Why are you shouting at me?"

"Sorry, I can't do anything. He is married and-" the buzzer to my flat goes, "one sec..." I walk over, pick up the phone on the intercom and see the outline of a man I don't know. "Hello?"

"Hello, is that Daisy, Daisy Wilkinson?" the man probed.

"Who's this?"

"My name is Vincent, and I am from the Daily Newspaper-"

"Nope!" I slam the intercom phone down.

"Shite, Daisy," My sister declares from the video phone, "check out your bedroom window. You can see the street below from there."

I slowly open the window, trying to be a stealth ninja, but it's one creaky stubborn fucker. Finally, I have it open enough to shove my head through and peer down from my second-floor flat and fuck my life. There are several reporters out there; they see me and start taking photos.

"Shit," I say, retreat my head, bang it on the frame and slam down the window.

"Are there loads?" Cora asks. I rub my head.

"Several!" I squeak.

"Shite!"

"Cora, what the hell am I going to do? I am on shift tomorrow, and they're here. They can't be here. I don't want to be in the paper, and I don't want to lose my job," I start to panic and instantly regret the kiss last night. Stupid vagina getting excited about Taron. Why couldn't you have been satisfied with Daniel? But no, and now look what trouble you have got me into!

"Wait for a second. I have an idea..." she muffles and speaks to Zach. I stare at myself in the mirror in my wardrobe, cursing myself for being such a tart and not having any restraint. But with Taron, I can't seem to hold it in, any of it. The chemistry is shit hot and I don't know how to deal with him. Cora comes back onto the video. "Okay, why don't you stay at our house? We are off to Italy tomorrow morning and we are gone for a week; the house is empty. Bring Kevin, just don't let him wee on the carpet OR sleep in the bed!"

Yeah, I can't promise either of those things.

Paparazzi really do suck
- Taron

JAMES BAY – LET IT GO

Half awake, half asleep, I'm tasting Daisy in my lucid dreams with her hot mouth on mine. I can feel my arousal and instinctively begin stroking. It feels so good, she feels so good, I need a release. That kiss last night pushed me over the edge to wanting so much more with her. Her kiss, our kiss, is something that would win Oscars in movies. That kiss was all-consuming, and I snapped and couldn't hold back anymore. After last night, I wanted to inhale all things Daisy, but she pushed me away. I wanted to push her up onto the vanity, roll up her dress, slide my hands up her soft legs, get down on my knees and put my mouth on her pussy. I would have licked her hard and deep until she moaned my name and came all over my face. I want to do so many naughty things with her. I would slip one finger in as I lick along her clit, and she would beg for more as I push in two fingers, hard and deep, fast and powerful. I would lick faster, suck harder; she would scream my name as she came all over my mouth again, and, with that image, I come all over myself.

"Shit," I mutter. I'm wide awake now, I lean over to the bedside table and grab some tissues, wiping away my Daisy fantasy because it would never be true. She would never be mine; I did not know how to escape this. I didn't even know if she wanted me.

Ask her then.

I throw the tissues across the room, and they land in the small bin by the door. Pleased with my aim, I hide back under the sheets. Seeing that it is only 8 a.m. and I don't have training until midday with my personal trainer, I am going to have a lie-in. I don't know if it is something I do. It's not something I have done yet, but it's the right decision. Maybe I can think of that kiss all over again, trying to imagine what Daisy would look like naked.

The door opens with a bang, then slams shut. My sheets are thrown from the guest bed. A paper smacks me in the face causing my eyes to fling open. Only to see Melissa full of rage, hands on hips. She looks tired and furious, not a look I've seen on her yet.

"Explain!" she shouts at me. I sit up, grab my glasses and look at the front cover of the newspaper.

"Fuck," I mutter.

"Explain!" She shouts louder. I look at my wife. What can I say? The truth is difficult. This situation of ours is unique, I did not know or love this woman. I had tried so hard to be what she needed, what she wanted. "Please," she whispers, tears fall freely down her face, and I feel like an utter shit for making her sad, for making her cry.

"I am sorry...I won't lie to you, Melissa...I kissed her," I have to be honest; she deserves that at least - mortification flitters on her face.

"Who is she?" Melissa pleads.

"Daisy...the paramedic...she-"

"The one that was there when you had your heart attack?" I nod. Anger and sadness contort her face.

"Why? Why Taron? We were happy...you are not this person...I don't even know who you are anymore," she starts to sob.

"Neither do I," I admit. I want to hold her and say sorry, but I wouldn't mean it. I'm not sorry for what I did with Daisy, I can't help how I feel.

"Why did you not even try with us? You said that some of your memories have come back?" Melissa's voice croaked.

"Some, yes, but not of you. Melissa, I have tried. I have tried so hard to be this person for you and it's not me. I can't be who you want me to be." The confession feels like a weight is slowly lifting from my shoulders.

"I have been patient, Taron; I have respected your boundaries. I thought we were making progress, and you kissed someone else. The media have splashed it everywhere. I am so embarrassed," she confesses. Her body is all crumpled and her head hangs low.

I look at Melissa, I don't know what she wants me to say. I have royally fucked up, I know, but I can't help how I feel. I didn't mean to kiss Daisy last night, but we had such a lovely evening. I laughed so hard my stomach ached and I hadn't smiled or laughed like that since I don't know when, and definitely not with Melissa. Daisy made me happy; I felt relaxed with her, and life was short. I know that from nearly dying. I wanted to seize the moment last night and fuck the consequences. I wanted to give into my desires, to give in to this sexual pull, I wanted to give in and do something to make me happy; that made me feel good and it felt so right kissing her.

But that came to kick me in my butt today. I didn't even see any paparazzi. It must have been one of the guests or something. I have ruined whatever this is between Daisy and I before it has even started. I can't have my wife; I can't have Daisy. What the hell am I supposed to do?

"I'm sorry, Melissa, I didn't plan any of this; it just happened. I bumped into her by accident," Melissa let out a sinister chuckle as if I was lying to her, but I don't blame her. What reason has she to trust this person that neither of us knows?

"I think...I think we need some space until we figure out what we both want," she finally says with sadness in her voice.

"I..." fuck this is hard. "I think we should break up."

"What?" Her eyes bulge with my confession and she blows out a breath.

"It's not working, I don't feel things for you that I should as a husband...I'm sorry," I look away for a moment, but I need to say this to her face and not be a coward.

"And that's it? But you feel these things...for her?"

"Yes." She lets out a slight gasp, clutching her stomach as if she is going to vomit. She takes a step back, out of the room and slams the door.

I lie back on the bed and let out a groan, "Fuck."

Well, at least it is out in the open now.

I abandoned my lie-in and took a long shower instead, thinking about how to talk to Melissa rationally and try to make her understand that I did not want to hurt her, but this was the best option for both of us. Even if Melissa couldn't see it now, she would. I wouldn't want someone to stay in a relationship with me if they didn't have any feelings. I emerge from the bedroom and walk downstairs to the kitchen. There is a note on the side from Melissa.

Taron,

I cannot believe that this is happening, I have no words and am incredibly hurt. I'm going to stay with my sister for a while, take care, M X

Even in her goodbye note, she is kind. I let out a sigh and make some coffee. I look at the paper and see the picture that was taken of us last night. Daisy looks so beautiful. No wonder I couldn't stop myself. No sane man could have, and now I have to pay the price.

But first, I need to find her.

The past, part 1 - Daisy

BEA MILLER — FEEL SOMETHING

I woke up at 4.30 a.m. drenched in sweat. I had another nightmare about Stefan; they didn't happen very often anymore, but when they did, they were bad. Either he was chasing me, or I was reliving the encounters we had whilst his head spun around like the girl in the film The Exorcist.

Stefan Routledge, the shithead that ruined me when I was sixteen.

I know why he had wiggled into my brain; it was seeing Sophie again last week. Whenever I looked at her, I thought of Stefan, and even when I didn't want to, I saw a little of him in Hope. Even after all these years, you would think that I would be over that, over him, and on the surface, I'm over it and over him, but scratch beneath it, I wasn't over it at all.

His face haunted me for years; he broke my confidence and self-esteem, and he made me feel worthless. It all happened seven years ago when Cora, Dad and I had returned home to England from living abroad in Dubai. I was a hormonal, naïve sixteen-year-old girl, and when I locked eyes with Stefan Routledge at school, I think my heart exploded. I really started to understand the word 'sexually turned on and frustrated.' I had gone to the music room to ask Cora to give me a lift home; at the time, she was in sixth form. My period had decided to make an early show, and they were relentless the first few days. The monthly joy of being a grown-up was a killer, and if I didn't change every few hours, I was leaking. It was definitely something like a car crash of disaster; my face would break out in spots, I felt frumpier, and binge ate more than normal. All these things made me miserable and a massive moody bitch. I waited outside the room for Cora to finish her music lesson, and Stefan strode out of the room; he walked with confidence, his face was luscious, and as he walked past, he looked at me. Not a brief hello, like, really looked at me. The look that says you're beautiful, the look that says I am interested, the look you want 'that' boy to give you. I smiled, and he smiled back, lifting his head in acknowledgement. Usually, I was the fat girl or the one that blended into the background, but at that moment, he made me feel beautiful.

"You're Daisy, right?" The fact that he knew my name made my heart flutter to the sky. Not only had he looked at me, but he also knew my name; someone who is two years older than me (who's smoking hot) knows me. I was impressed, giddy with excitement and I was already obsessed.

"That's right," I answered, trying to sound cool, but my voice definitely cracked at the end.

Bugger.

"Nice," he responds, licking his lips slightly as if he wanted to eat me. He flashes his cute smile and walks away. I broke out in a hot flush immediately because no one had given me attention like that before, and it felt amazing.

But they say that the devil wears many masks.

After that encounter, I was all in. I made sure to come to most of Cora's music lessons and wait like a good little girl. I was making up some shit or another of why I needed to be there. I wore shorter skirts. tighter tops, more make-up, styled my hair better and seen as the shirts at that school wore pretty much see-through; I wore a lacy pink bra so he could really see my boobs, I had great breasts, and I was not afraid to use them.

A few weeks later, things changed. We continued the whole smiling at one another, him saying 'hi and 'Daisy, looking fit today' and me responding, 'You would know.' Just those few encounters made me feel confident and sexy. He made me feel nervous, but in a good way, and it started to make me feel sad that I had never kissed anyone. But I was so excited that Stefan could be my first kiss, my first love. The problem was that I had never initiated anything like this, I was on the path of the unknown, and I didn't know how to approach Stefan Routledge.

But he did.

He seemed to leave early this particular lesson. I don't know why, but maybe he knew I would be there. He looked at me as he closed the door behind him.

"Pink suits you," he commented and started to walk away. I knew he meant my bra, and then I felt annoyed that I wasn't confident enough to go after what I wanted. He stops halfway down the hall, "I gotta go, Daisy. Are you coming?"

Fuck yeah!

"Sure," I answered in a non-committal voice.

"Were you waiting for someone?" He asks, starting to walk away, and I walk after him at a quick pace.

"Just you," I answer boldly—high-fiving my inner self for the quick boost of confidence.

"Were you now?" He gives me that look that makes my insides quiver and turn to mush. I felt my cheeks pink, and a lot of blood rush to my vagina because we were going somewhere *together.*

This was it; this was the day we kissed and became boyfriend and girlfriend.

We walk across the car park, and I get into this old beat-up car; it smells horrible, like bad, boy odour and definitely weed. He starts the car and pulls out of the car park. I feel bad for ditching school and I will fake an illness to Dad later because I am not missing this chance. The chance to be with him. He drives for a few minutes until I realise, I don't know where we are going.

"Stefan," he doesn't answer me straight away as if lost in his own thoughts; he hums a response. "Where are we going?"

"Pick up," he murmurs. His car driving skills are pretty shit, he drives far too fast, and I swear he runs through a few red lights. I want to feel a little scared, but the excitement that I'm with Stefan alone washes that feeling away.

"What's a pick-up?" He doesn't answer, and I am unsure if I have offended him or if he thinks I am stupid for not knowing what he is talking about. A few minutes later, he slows to a stop in the next village to school, not somewhere I have been before, and I look at the bungalow we have stopped outside; it looks a little run down. I go to get out of the car. Stefan puts his hand on my leg to stop me. I look back at him, confused.

"No, Daisy, *you* stay here, in the car," the way he says it makes me feel like a child. He gets out and jogs to the small bungalow knocks on the cracked painted door and then walks in. I take out my phone and ring my dad. He picks up after two rings.

"Daisy?" He answers with concern, he knows I should be in a lesson and not calling him.

I put on a croaky voice, "Dad, I have had to go home. I am not well."

"Oh no, did you sign out with student services? They didn't ring me?"

"Sorry, Dad, I forgot. It was a terrible migraine, and I had just to leave," I should feel bad for lying, but I don't.

Daisy," his voice is stern, "You can't just leave school like that. I can get into trouble," he sighs, "I will sort it out, go to bed. I'm home late tonight, so I will call you in a bit. I will let Cora know, and she can check in on you when she gets home."

"Love you, Dad," I whisper.

"Love you too, sweet pea." I sit in Stefan's car for 32 minutes; I sit there and think what a stupid person I am for waiting; I am getting angrier by the minute. How long am I expected to wait? Should I just leave? But then he appears all smiles and gets back in the car. He smells like pot.

"Stefan, I have waited for a really long time; what took you so long?" I look at him, bubbling with anger, and he leans over, his eyes hooded and kisses me. His kiss surprises me. His lips are soft and warm, and his tongue is in my throat before I have fully opened my mouth. His mouth tasted like an ashtray, but I didn't mind; it was really wet but erotic, and Stefan. He pulls back and looks at me.

"Have you ever kissed someone before, Daisy?" he muses.

"Erm, yeah..." he raises his eyebrows at me, and I look away, "No," he scoffs a little.

"I can tell." Hurt radiates my whole body. Was I that bad? How can you tell if someone hasn't had a proper kiss before? He strokes the side of my face and makes me look at him.

"Don't worry, baby," he coos, "I won't tell anyone." He leans in and kisses me again, and I want to kiss him the way he wants me to, but I don't know how; he's made me feel stupid and unkissable. But if it's that bad, why is he kissing me again? I will practice with my pillow tonight and see if I can get the technique right. I don't want to be a bad kisser. I try to relax more this time and ease my tongue into his mouth, which I think he likes as he groans, so I must be getting better at this. He pulls back; he's so close I can see the flex of green in his baby-blue eyes.

"Let's see these amazing tits of yours then Daisy. The pink bra has been staring at me for ages now," I giggle at his silly joke until he puts his hand under my shirt. I smack his hand away.

"No, Stefan, I am not showing you my boobs," I pull back and glare at him, staring out of the window and crossing my arms. He huffs.

"My god, Daisy, calm down; being a bad kisser and frigid will not do well for you." Tears pool in my eyes immediately. This was not how I expected him to be, I thought he liked me. I thought he might ask to be my boyfriend; I wasn't ready to show him my boobs; we'd only just kissed.

"Drive me home, Stefan, now!" Do not cry, Daisy. He lets out a groan and a sigh. Starts the car and drives me home.

The past, part 2 - Daisy

LAUV - THE STORY NEVER ENDS

I wish I could say that was my only encounter with Stefan Routledge, but it was not, and as a sucker for punishment, I went back for more the following week. He kept giving me cute smiles in the hallway at school the following day. For some reason, we seemed to pass each other on the way to different lessons when usually it was me chasing him. The day after that, he put a little note in my hand with the word 'Sorry' and a love heart. Later that day, he walked with me down the hallway to my lesson and linked his pinky to mine, and I thought this was okay; I thought this was love. By the 3rd day, all was forgiven, and I caved as he asked me to meet him near the bike sheds at the back of the school. And like a lamb to slaughter, I did.

As I arrived, he was there, leaning against the enclosure, smoking weed. He looked fucking gorgeous with his tight t-shirt, tight jeans, converse and floppy brown hair. When he saw me, his eyes lit up, and he flicked his fag end away. He waved me to the side, and I momentarily realised how secluded and private this area was. He pulled me into a hug, and I loved every second of it; the thought was forgotten as all I wanted was to be his. But I didn't know what that was, what that would entail.

Maybe this is when he asks to be my boyfriend.

"I missed you," he confesses. I feel my body mold into his, and I love how he fits into my arms. But what I should have been asking was all the questions, such as why? Do you even know me? But I smiled a happy one; his attention gave me all the best butterflies. He kissed me again, slowly, carefully. He wrapped his arms around me, deepening the kiss and easing his tongue into me. This kiss was better, sexy and romantic. I moved my arms around him and breathed in his coconut scent.

The kissing on my pillow definitely paid off.

This kiss was the one I imagined; apart from the ash taste from his mouth, it was perfect. He pulled me closer, "Feel what you do to me, Daisy," he murmured over the kiss and moved my hand around and put it on to his hard-on over his jeans. This was the first time I had ever felt a penis; they didn't scare me or anything. It was a surprise how big they got and how forward Stefan was being again. I went to move my hand away, but he kept his hand on top of mine. "Daisy, don't be a cock tease. You know how much I want you?"

Did I? I felt uneasy, uncomfortable. Is this what I had to do for him to be my boyfriend?

He unbuckles his jeans and pulls them down slightly. "I really want you to touch me, Daisy," he kisses me again, deeper, more urgent, as if kissing me is what he needed to do to convince me. "You turn me on so much," he adds. He removed his hand and guided mine under his boxers. And even though I felt uncomfortable, and this wasn't what I wanted to do, I let him put my hand into his boxers, and I grasped his penis. I held it for a moment, and he placed a small kiss on my lips, encouraging me to continue. I moved my hand slightly up and down in what we had been shown with masturbation in a sex ed class, but also what I had seen on porn sites. "Not too tight, Daisy. Let me help you." He puts his hand over mine again as I go to move it away.

"Stefan," I whisper, "I don't really feel comfortable," I admit. He chuckles as if I am joking.

"Don't be silly, Daisy, this is natural," he moves my hand with his again, and his eyes become hooded. I look around, wondering if I can get away, wondering if someone would see us. Stefan notices, "No one is coming here, Daisy; well, I will be in a minute," he moves my hand up and down some more and starts to make grunting noises. I feel sick; this isn't what I imagined being with him would be like at all. He moves his hand away and starts to undo my top.

"What are you doing?" I gasped, moving his hand away.

"I'm going to come on your perfect tits, Daisy," he looks at me undeterred.

"No, Stefan," I put my arms in a cross shape over my breasts - as if that would have helped, if that would have stopped him.

"Yes, Daisy," his voice is cold, "otherwise people are going to think you are frigid, and you will be the laughing stock of the school. You don't want that now, do you, Daisy?"

He removes my arms slowly, keeping eye contact with me as mine becomes glassy. As he undid my shirt, revealing my pink lacy bra, he appraised my breasts with a dirty smile, and a tear escaped my eye. He lightly touches the top of my bra, and I look down at the floor, feeling disappointment in myself, humiliation spreading through my body. But mainly, I'm ashamed of letting him do this to me. He pushes my shoulders down so that I am almost crouching, he takes his erect cock, continues for a few moments fisting his own cock, and he leans back slightly, groaning as he releases himself over the top of my boobs; it then it dribbles down into my bra. He leans over me, pulling my chin up to look at him with a sneer. He uses the pad of his thumb to roughly push away my tear.

"You know, Daisy, you shouldn't dress like a fat slut if you don't want people to do things like this to you. I mean, what do you expect when you dress like that and have it all on show? You should be careful with yourself." He slips his penis back into his boxers and pulls his trousers up. He lights up a cigarette and walks away. I pull my top back up and button it, not bothering to wipe away the mess. I put my blazer over the top, something I rarely wear as it is uncool, even if it is the school's policy stating that one should be worn at all times.

I walk back to the music block quickly, knowing that's where the nearest toilets are and the opposite direction to where Stefan went. I hurry through the corridor and zone into the toilet door at the end of it. The next thing I know, I'm on the floor. I look up to see Mr Jones (Zach) looking horrified at what has just happened.

"Oh, Daisy, I'm so sorry, I didn't look where I was going," he holds out his hand to help me up, and the thought of touching another man again brings bile to my throat; I ignore his kind gesture and get up myself. "Are you okay?" I nod without looking at him. "Are you sure?" I start to walk away. "Daisy, do you know where Stefan is?" I stop in my tracks and look down, letting out a small sob, a weakness I will not show again, emotions that I will not feel again for any man. I hear Mr. Jones's (Zach) footsteps approach, and he stands in front of me. "Daisy, are you sure you are okay?" his voice is full of concern, but I dismiss it immediately.

"Just feel sick, sir," I spit out as I run to the toilet.

I often think then, if only I had said something, could I have changed the future, changed other's fate. It's a thought that often burdens my soul.

But one thing I do know is that day, I changed as a person.

Undercover - Daisy

SIA - HELIUM

I hide out at Cora and Zach's house for the next week; she was on her honeymoon in Italy. The pictures of her, Zach and Amy eating pizza, in Venice on a gondola, at Lake Como on a boat ride, and in Rome on the bus tours make me insanely jealous. But her honeymoon came at a great time as I did some sort of mission-impossible escape from my apartment. Sunglasses and baseball caps do not work for hiding out from the media. They're like fricking sharks smelling blood from a mile away, the buggers.

I had to drive around like a prat for several hours before they got bored, and then I finally drove to Cora and Zach's. Good job that I have a clad iron bladder and a love for driving with the right playlist. I went with Harry Styles mixed in with some Queen and topped it off with 911, screaming/yelling the words to some firm favourites; it was great. I'm not sure Kevin liked it much – but he's used to my singing now.

I like Cora and Zach's place, a cute little townhouse just outside of London, right by these amazing sunflower and lavender fields. Even at night, you can smell the lavender on the breeze; no wonder everyone is so chill that lives here. I'm on day two of being undercover, but I have to head back into London as I promised to take Cole to the airport. I rock up, text Cole I'm here and wait. I am not getting out of the car, just in case the media descends, but it makes me giggle as I feel like his own personal driver. The drive is just under an hour from London to Luton Airport, so it's not that bad, and I needed to get out of the house today. Even if it's only been a few days, sitting in the house gets boring really fast.

"I am worried about you, Daisy?" Cole admits as we hit the M1. I know traffic won't be too bad on a Monday lunchtime, thank goodness.

"Why?" his question makes me feel sad, as he doesn't need to worry about me.

"You seem different, nervous; everything okay?"

"Yes, no, I don't know. Things have been intense," I admit.

"I read in the paper about you and that footballer," I sit quietly for a moment; Cole is the closest I have had to a dad since he passed, so his opinion and thoughts mean a lot to me. "Look, I am a very relaxed person, and I have always supported you both despite whatever mischief you have got into..."

"But?"

"I don't know Daisy. Something feels off with Taron, I have this bad feeling, but I can't put my finger on it. What I am saying is, be careful, people with that kind of money and power, it usually comes at a price," he confesses, "which you seem to be paying for already."

I feel so annoyed with his comments. He didn't even know Taron or how I felt. I sit there silently stewing, and by the time we have driven up to departures drop-off, I really feel like throwing him out. I pull up into the layby so that he can get out.

"Don't be upset by my comment, darling. I am expressing how I feel and it only comes from a place of love. All I ever wanted, all Edward ever wanted, was for you to be happy." I smile, and some of my anger dissolves. I know he's only looking out for me. "Are you...happy?"

"I want to be, desperately, career-wise, yes. Love life is shit," I admit.

"Do you think Taron is someone you could love?" he asks.

"Maybe," he smiles, and we hug awkwardly in the car.

"I love you, Daisy. I will text when I land, and you better come out and see me for Christmas," he moans.

"I will book the flights this week," he kisses me fondly on the cheek and exits the car.

I let Cole's words float around my mind as I drive back to Zach and Cora's house. I think a nap will sort me out, as I have called in sick for a few days whilst the crap from the media blows over. I have only just gotten back from taking Cole to the airport when there's a knock on the door. In two minds to open it, I pause for a moment in case it's the media, but then the knock comes again, harder this time, and I hear Jay on the other side muttering profanities to himself – Kevin is barking like an insane dog.

"You are not sick," he declares when I open the door and he barges his way uninvited.

"Hi Jay, what a surprise. Please do come in," I mock whilst shutting the door. I follow him to the kitchen.

"Kevin," he beckons, with which he comes over happily for a visitor stroke; I think he has been a bit bored with only my company. Jay gives him all the love and a lot of treats. "Make me a cuppa then," he asks cheekily. I pop the kettle on and make us tea, pulling out some biscuits because this conversation is going to need sugar and a dip-and-dunk biscuit session. He joins me at the table once I have put everything out. We sit in silence for a few minutes. "You are not sick." I sigh and roll my eyes.

"You know I am not sick, Jay. I just want to crawl into a hole and not be seen by journalists. They are crazy."

He laughs, "Serves you right for kissing Mr Fancy Pants."

I smirk, "Not helping." We sit in silence for a few minutes as I inhale some custard creams and chocolate digestives. The diet is out the window again.

Was I even on a diet? Probably not.

"Look, the only way to face it is to face it." I roll my eyes again at him.

"Not helping." He puts his hand over mine.

"Are you okay?" his voice filled with concern.

I smile. "Yes, I am. Thank you for coming," I admit. Jay constantly reminds me what an unconditional friend is and what it means. He didn't need to come and check on me, but he did because he wanted to, and that makes me feel all kinds of grateful to have him as a friend.

"You're welcome, so you are doing your shift tonight, then?" I groan.

"Please don't make me," I whine.

"You are on shift with me. It will be fine; I will be your protector," he flexes his muscles, and I laugh, "Get it all out. Once the media gets bored, they move on. Just show them you are not bothered and your usual boring self."

"But I am bothered; that is why I am hiding, Jay." He looks at me for a moment.

"You know he turned up at the hospital yesterday asking for you," he admits with a glint in his eye.

My mouth opens in shock, "Shut up. No, he did not." Why would he be looking for me? It didn't make sense. I told him we could not be together.

Jay nods, "He did. He also said he was there for an appointment," he uses his fingers as quotation marks as if he didn't believe Taron was there for an appointment at all.

"What did you say?" I ask. I try not to seem bothered, but he knows I am hanging on every word he says.

"I said you were sick..."

"And?" I am on the edge of my seat; he seems to be dragging out this story on purpose.

"He seemed sad; he asked for your number, to which I told him no, and he left."

"Oh," I felt happy he had asked about me and now I am cross again because he has a wife. But he asked for my number, which made me feel excited, and then cross all over again because he has a wife!

"And this," Jay adds and puts down a newspaper.

"Jay, I am not reading that shit; it's been giving me anxiety. If I don't read it, it hasn't happened."

"That's very childish, Daisy, but you might want to read this," he unfolds the paper and shows me the headlines.

"Premier League footballer Taron and wife Melissa split," I read out loud, "he broke up with her?" I scan the paper and see that from an anonymous source, Melissa moved out and is staying with family, and they've asked to respect their privacy at this time. "Shit."

I feel that bubbling again in my body; I'm excited and angry again, but now for different reasons. Had Taron broken up with her, or had she broken up with him? Did he want my number to tell me he wanted to be with me? Or did he ask for my number so that he could agree with what I had said in the bathroom and that this 'relationship' could not go any further?

Not knowing anything makes me feel incredibly frustrated. Jay has the biggest smile on his face; he knows me so well, and I am itching to find out. He knew that this would happen.

"Yep, so home wrecker, get your ass back to work this evening; otherwise, I am telling the papers where you are hiding out, so you'll never get a break." I look at him with my pissed-off face.

"You wouldn't," I stare coldly at him as he grins, scoffing his face with more biscuits.

"Try me," he says, daring me to find out.

For fuck's sake. He so would tell the press where to find me.

Bastard.

Back to work - Daisy

TAKE THAT - BABE

I have to admit that Jay was right; the first part of my shift wasn't too bad. The journalists were there, but I stood and answered their questions, smiled like a Cheshire cat and they mostly left so I could get on and do my job. The questions were stupid: how did I feel about the breakup? Were me and Taron together? Had I spoken to Taron? I think they were disappointed that I couldn't give them anything juicy, because the worst part of this is that I did not know anything either; the press probably knew more than me.

Jay has just nipped to the toilet whilst I finish checking in with the Accident and Emergency receptionist. The poor patient had a fall down the stairs, with a suspected broken hip, which is one of the worst kinds of breaks to get when he's a man in his 80s. I shiver and feel that there are eyes on me. I turn, concerned that the media may have gotten bold and wandered in, but instead, I see that Taron is in the waiting room.

"Shit," I mutter.

"Loverboy is here," Jay whispers, suddenly emerging next to me. I nudge him, he laughs and looks at his watch. "We've got about five minutes before we need to clean down the truck; I will finish the handover with the patient. Go and see what he wants. Even I can see that he is hurting." I lock eyes with Taron, and he approaches cautiously with a slight smile.

"Hi," he says softly. I tentatively smile back, "Can we talk?" I nod and lead him into one of the side rooms, praying that the journalists have gone and have not captured this encounter on camera. Thankfully, the Triage room is empty. I gesture to him to go inside and I shut the door behind us. I sigh.

"Taron, why are you here?" He clears his throat and licks his lips and jeez, why is he so fricking beautiful?

Great, clear thinking, Daisy.

"I came here because I wanted to ask you out," he says confidently.

"What?" I reply, surprised.

"On a date," he adds.

"No, Taron," I declare.

"Just hear me out. Look, I know how we met isn't conventional, but I can't help the way I feel; I like you, Daisy, a lot. You are in all my thoughts, and how can such a wonderful feeling be wrong?"

"Taron, we can't..." I look away, unsure what to say or what to do.

"I left Melissa. I told her about us," I turn to him, in shock. He left her for me. I can't help but feel a little excited by this news and terrible at the same time. I see the sadness in his eyes, too.

"What?!" I cry, "Oh fuck!" He comes closer, which is such a bad idea on so many levels, but I can feel it, the need to be near him, the pull between us, to kiss him, to have him deep inside of me, and I can't seem to stop him. I put out my hand as a warning to stay on his side of the room, but he takes it as an invitation to come closer.

"Don't be mad; I can't be with someone I feel nothing for; I can't live a lie. Life is too short for that," he gently places his hands on the side of my arms and rubs his fingertips soothingly up and down; shivers explode over my body.

He needs to stop touching me, or my willpower is going to be on the floor.

"I want to be with you, Daisy." His brutal, honest confession has me quivering; he's so close to me that I can't think clearly. His breath is hot on my face, and I close my eyes briefly to try and understand what is going on. I feel his lips gently brush against mine as if he is testing me. "Do you want to be with me, Daisy?"

Oh boy, I really did. I want him, all of him.

"I can't, Taron, I don't want to be a homewrecker." He kisses me gently on the lips, his manly scent filling my nose, short wiring any sense or coherent thoughts in my head.

"You are not a homewrecker, Daisy. You are mine." His gravelled, demanding voice has me melting. When he gently kisses me again, I kiss him back. I wrap my arms around his neck, and he pulls me closer as his arms twist around my back. His tongue is immediately deep in my mouth and I groan into his. If he's this good with his mouth on mine, I am excited about what he can do with that tongue of his down on my clit! The kiss becomes hotter and heavier, and he picks me up and places me on the desk. He pushes my legs open and stands between my legs and runs his fingers through my hair, such a gentle but loving gesture. I feel his erection against my stomach, and the urge is there to stick my hands down his trousers, to lick and suck him so hard that he comes into my mouth. All these dirty thoughts flit across my mind when he's close and his lips are on mine; it has me humming and moaning into his mouth like I want to eat him for dinner.

My phone goes, alerting me to the next emergency call and I pull away begrudgingly.

"I have to go, Taron," I whisper over his soft lips.

"Wait, before you go, can I have your number?" I laugh and nod. I put my number into his phone, he dials it, and I hear mine ring. He gives me that dirty smirk and walks out of the room. "I will be seeing you, Daisy."

Jay cocks his head around the door, assessing the situation, "That looked like fun!" He laughs, my cheeks feel hot, hell my whole body is on fire. "You going to be able to walk to the van?" I giggle.

"Yes, you dipshit, let's go."

The next few hours of the shift fly by, and I can't keep a smile from emerging on my face. I park the van up in Accident and Emergency space with an abdominal pain patient. From all our tests, we are unsure of what it might be: appendicitis, twisted bowel, who knows, but the man is in pain, and the whole van and streets we drove through knew about it. He definitely is not good with pain, and I am not great with loud noises. I am relieved when he's booked in and the doctors take him away. Jay nips up to the staffroom to refill our flasks full of tea whilst I clean down the van – hopefully, he brings back biscuits, too.

"Are you Daisy?" I continue cleaning the van, I can't be bothered with any more of the media tonight. If I carry on being 'boring' as Jay says, such as wiping down the inside of the ambulance van, then this lady reporter can get bored and bugger off too.

"That's me," I answer whilst spraying down the stretcher.

"I'm Melissa." I stop cleaning and turn to her. Her face looks a cross between sadness and anger, and my stomach drops. I caused that; I did that. I step out of the van and face her because she deserves to see me. I have to hear what she has to say despite feeling a little scared and guilty.

She slaps me across the cheek hard. A proper soap opera smack and the noise is a lot louder than I expected it to be, too. I gasp at the feeling and hold my cheek, looking at her in shock.

"You bitch, you've ruined my life," she declared venomously. I lower my head in defeat.

"I'm sorry," I whisper.

"You will be," she laughs, "you're not even his type," I look up as she scowls at me and wrinkles her perfect porcelain doll face as if she is smelling something rotten. At that moment, I let all the emotions consume me from this ridiculous situation, and she made me feel fat and ugly in comparison to her. She lets out a frustrated groan and stomps away.

I don't blame her, though, she's right, I am a bitch.

I can play - Taron

ED SHEERAN - REMEMBER THE NAME

My phone alarm blares out at me. I roll over and turn it off. It is 8 a.m., and I feel exhausted. I couldn't sleep last night as I was too excited. I had a phone call yesterday from my manager. He asked if I wanted to 'play' in the friendly charity match today and I was all in. I wasn't technically allowed to play, but my manager said that if there were any free kicks, he could sub me in, to play. It is a charity match and all sorts of celebrities will be playing, so it is only a bit of fun. But he also said that the world needed to see how miraculous my recovery has been, how I was still an excellent striker, and it would be great coverage for the charity they were raising money for; the press would eat it up, and so would my sponsors. But even if it weren't for any of those reasons, I am all in any way.

I'm so desperate to get back onto the pitch; it makes my whole body hurt. My doctor advised against it, obviously. She said I needed to wait the whole 12 weeks before getting into more vigorous exercise and reminded me that my insurance wouldn't cover it because I hadn't been signed off yet. She also reminded me that it was only three more weeks to wait, even if my progress had been more positive than she imagined, but I didn't listen. Some of the players remarked that I was getting back to my old self, and I didn't even know it, so apparently, I am hot-headed and stubborn.

Good to know.

I get out of bed with ease and turn on the shower, I am staying at a hotel near the football ground. I left 'my house' last week, telling Melissa that she should live there as it didn't feel like my home anyway; she should have it – it's the least I could do for all the pain I have caused her. I didn't get a response, but I know she is back living there. The reporters are giving me a daily running commentary on everything. I have texted Melissa a few times to ask how she is, but she hasn't replied, and I don't blame her either. She probably hates my guts, so I am happy to give her the space she needs.

I let the hot water ease away any tension I am carrying. I love this hotel; it feels more like my home. I feel more settled here since I left the hospital and, despite the shitstorm I have created, I feel happy. Being so near to the football ground keeps me motivated, I'm vigilant with my physio and my training. This week, I have started with slow jogging and a few kilograms of weight. I feel my body becoming stronger each day, and that is all I can ask for.

Except my memory is still fucked!

I hadn't seen Daisy since our kiss last week at the hospital, but we have texted or spoken most days. She is funny, smart, and beautiful. I could feel myself falling in love with her. I texted her last night and asked if she would come to the game. I really wanted her to come and watch me today; her watching me play or even her just sitting in the stand makes me feel important, and I want her to be a part of today. After my shower, I text Daisy again:

Hey, I really hope you are coming today, I know you have read my message and not responded. I get that it's all a bit scary with the media, but I really want you to be there, please, T x

I am annoyed she hadn't replied already. Why is she making me wait? I want her to come to watch me. I want her to see me for who I am and understand my life now. I get it if she doesn't want to come as the press will be there, and they're like a swarm of flies, but this is my life, and if she couldn't cope with it, how would this relationship work?

I have also had a lot of shit from some of the players about what a dick I have been to Melissa, but what could I say? I know I had been. I got the whole team together the other day, and we all sat and hashed it out. Not that I needed to explain myself, but I knew that this was important. As a football team, we work as just that: a team. So, if one of us isn't getting on, then there's no unity within it and I can't be the one who breaks us down. I have already done that by having this heart condition; because of me, this team has already lost so much. So, I had to be honest, I had to tell them exactly what had happened. Some were okay, some weren't, but understood, and that's all I can ask from the team.

My team. It felt so good to say that.

I dress in my dark suit, trying to arrange the tie – I had to *YouTube* that one to do it properly, but what I really can't wait for is to put my footie kit on. I have walked the grounds a thousand times this week, roamed the corridors, and soaked in the atmosphere and the smell. I love my team; I love the way the place makes me feel. It makes me feel alive and important; I feel the love of it in my blood, my brain, and even my soul. I am about to leave when my phone buzzes from Daisy with one word:

Maybe

Well, that's better than a no. I decided to walk to the ground and kind of wished I hadn't. As I walk nearer to the ground, the media descends on me like a hive of bees. I take some deep breaths and answer as many questions as I can: how am I feeling about the match today, whether I'm sad because I couldn't play the whole match, and how Daisy is? I decide that honesty is the best policy and give them all the information that they need, stating that Daisy may be able to attend today. But the question that got me was, how does your wife, Melissa, feel about this? It makes me so sad - I feel like a bastard. I tell them that I am sorry for hurting her and that all I want is for her to be happy. Thank goodness that was the last question before I head into the ground. A few fans are outside the football ground, so I sign some autographs and smile for photos, which is nice.

I'm not too much of a bastard if the fans still like me.

I change into my football kit and drink in the excitement of the room, of the player's chatter and the team. I didn't know how I would play or what it would feel like, but I felt the anxiety and the nervousness building even more, in a good way. As the coach gives a speech and goes through the strategies, I relish the way I am feeling.

Content.

I sit on the bench and watch my team play; they are fantastic. I knew they were. I have watched all the games from the last season at least three times, poured over all the goals and the media coverage. My knowledge about my team right here is excellent, but seeing them live in action is something else; it's magical. I have even watched myself play on the reruns; I am bloody good, but did I still know how to play like that? Could I play like that?

Probably not.

After half-time, the score is still 0 - 0, but we have missed some good opportunities. There are several famous band members, celebrity chefs, TV soap stars and radio presenters playing and they're pretty good too. I have no clue who any of them are, but I smile politely and wave back if anyone looks my way. They all seem to be having a good time.

I look across the crowd, but I still haven't seen Daisy. I message her the seat numbers and send another text at halftime, but they remain empty. It makes me sad that she didn't want to be here, and it makes me realise that maybe I am more invested in this relationship than she is. I gave up Melissa to be with her, and I haven't asked her for anything. But the one thing I asked for, she couldn't do it or wouldn't do it. Suddenly I am all kinds of angry and pissed off.

I stand up from the bench, pull my head back in the game and shout at the referee as what I just witnessed was definitely a foul with the other team. The referee gives it, blowing his whistle and issuing a yellow card to the other team. The fans split evenly, either clapping or booing. It is the oddest noise and feeling. My manager nudges me, "Come on then, Taron, you're up; show the world what you are made of, son." I pull off my yellow jacket and do a couple of stretches whilst the linesman puts up his substitution board, calls in number 12 and me out on number 9. Everyone starts to clap and yell, and I feel my heartbeat going wild. Whilst finishing my last stretch, I close my eyes and take a calming breath.

Calm, Taron, you will be just fine.

I have a short flashback of Melissa saying these words to me. I don't know when or where, but I hear her voice. I shake the moment off; now is not the time to have a flashback. I high-five the player and take a slow jog onto the field, clapping with everyone else as they cheer me on. I take the football from the referee and go to the penalty box. I place it in the middle and look at the goalie; he looks shit scared. But then maybe that's my face reflecting back at him.

Taking a few steps back, I close my eyes again briefly and breathe; the noise of the crowd echoes out. I open my eyes, lock on the goalie, run towards the ball, move my eyes right and kick left, a tactic I have seen myself do a few times when watching my games back on television. The ball hit the top left-hand of the net, I scored a goal. The crowd goes wild. I punch the sky, "Yes," I cry. My teammates come over and hug me, ruffle my hair or pat me on the back. "I still got it."

It's a proud moment, another step towards recovery, and knowing that I have still got the skills in me somewhere to be a footballer is utter relief and joy. It is written all over my face. I look over to the empty seats.

But Daisy didn't want to come and see it.

The date - Daisy

One Direction - Little Things

After the incident at the football match last week, I was unsure about whether to pursue this relationship with Taron. It was one thing trying to date Taron, but it also meant dating the media, too. They were every-where. Jay's advice of showing you're boring is not working anymore now. The media had caught wind that Taron and I are 'an item.' They practically held me hostage for most of the game, firing off all kinds of questions I couldn't answer. They called me a lot of horrible names, and when they happily made me cry, they finally had enough of me, letting me go from their barbaric questioning. When I got to the turnstiles, the security wouldn't let me through. They said for safety reasons, they couldn't let any more fans in to watch the game due to overbooking. In the end, I gave up and went home miserable.

It didn't help either that my hormones were all over the place, I have had so many sexy dreams about Taron that it is disgusting. It's as if my body wants him all the time; it scares me and makes me feel a little mental about how he has invaded all of my thoughts. I think what is bothering me the most at the moment is whether I can live a life in the limelight as he does. The media hated me, fuck, I hated myself. But the media are awful; they call me a homewrecker, a slut, and fat (media words, but we can interpret them). Melissa had only lashed out once to the media about it. How heartbroken she was – the media were all on her side, obviously. But it is the pictures they are printing of her, where she looks sickly and not as perfect as I had seen her. Her friends were saying they were worried about her, and I felt terrible. My mental health was declining, so I rang Sophie for some advice.

"I have no answers, Daisy," Sophie says, "I couldn't deal with the media myself, so I ran away from it instead. That is not my advice, by the way, only what I did."

Should I run away?

Nevertheless, Sophie assures me that it will die down eventually and offers a free escape to her house in Manchester for a few weeks if I want. I politely thank her but decline. I realise that I can't run away because I think, even though the media is a bitch, I am more interested in how things might play out with Taron.

The what-ifs are a real bitch in life. My mistakes are easier to get over.

Taron is persistent and if his kisses were even a minor indication of what sex would be like with him, I am going to be the most pleasured I have ever been in my life, and that thought alone made me want to continue this. It's a war in my head that I struggle with; it's that song by the Clash, "Should I stay or should I go, 'If I go there will be trouble, and if I stay, it will be double', and that is where I sat.

There was no right answer to this question. So, I will do what I have never done before, I will follow my heart (and my vagina).

The buzzer to my apartment goes and I know it's Taron. I get up from the edge of my bed where I have been sitting for the last twenty minutes procrastinating about life. I take another look at myself in the long mirror. I am wearing a maxi dress with sandals, my hair is curly and I have gone for a natural look today with my makeup, lots of nude colours and light browns. I open the door to be greeted by the 6ft dark, handsome Greek god in a suit. He smells like manly pine and every dirty dream I have had about him for weeks. He hasn't shaved in a few days and has got the best damn stubble I have ever seen, and his suit, jeez, is deep blue and perfect. I think I would rather stay in now, rip his clothes off and feast on him instead. He takes my breath away.

He pulls out some flowers from behind his back, roses, very nice. I am not a flower person, but for him, I would be. He passes them to me, smiles, and then he gives me a kiss on the cheek. I'm pretty sure he's being very reserved because if he feels an inkling of how I feel right now, we will not make it out of the apartment, as I want to lick him like a Dip Dab lollipop!

"You look stunning, Daisy," he confesses. I smile and lay the flowers on the side table. Kevin has now realised that someone is at the door and comes bounding over. Taron looks down and smiles, stepping back and patting Kevin awkwardly on the head.

He doesn't like dogs.

This makes me sad. I pull Kevin gently by the collar, not wanting him to run out into the corridor, thinking it's time for his walk. But he seems happy to go back onto his bed if he is not receiving the attention, he probably thinks he deserves. I lay out his Kong treats, grabbing my bag and jacket from the side. Taron takes my hand as we walk to the elevator and I press the button. As soon as we step into the lift, Taron crowds me into the corner; he brushes my hair back, leaning into me and taking a deep breath.

"I don't know how I am going to keep my hands off you tonight," he whispers into my hair as I shudder with excitement. As we exit the lift and the lobby, he guides me to his car, and we both sit in the back. That's when I realise, he not only has a Rolls Royce but a driver that comes with it.

Wow!

As we are driven through London, I am grateful we are not in the car long because being with Taron alone sends all kinds of naughty thoughts to my brain. We sit in a comfortable silence; the seats are so soft I would doze off if I weren't so sexually frustrated. I realise we have been driven to Mayfair, pulling up outside of the Dorchester Hotel. As we walk in, I realise we are going to the French Michelin Restaurant of Alain Ducasse. I swear I might need to run in and change my knickers because this place is where food dreams are made of. They make rainbows into food here.

"I wanted to treat you to a nice dinner," he looks at me with a smile. I don't know why his comment confuses and annoys me, its as if he has to treat me to a lavish meal so that I will want to spend time with him. I didn't need to be treated; I just wanted him...alone...naked.

When we arrive at the restaurant, the waitress practically orgasms over Taron, talking his ear off. As we walk over to the table, there is a gentle hush across the restaurant and people, who I don't know are staring at me, and not that happy stare; it's a look of confusion and a little disgust. I want to run out of this restaurant and cry into a bowl of ice cream, but instead, I pull out my inner bitch and hold my head high – sticking my tongue out at one snotty-looking couple.

As we walk to the centre of the restaurant, there is a magical, luminescent oval curtain; it is a beautiful and unique centrepiece that makes the whole restaurant glimmer and shine. The waitress pulls some of the lights aside and beckons us in. Taron looks at me with a knowing smile and my jaw hits the floor. I pull Taron back gently on the arm and whisper, "We are eating in here?"

"I wanted some privacy, but somewhere exclusive, just for us," he whispers back.

We sit and the waitress hands us both a menu, smiling and shoving her boobs slightly in Taron's face. I shouldn't be bothered by this peacock of a display because this is who he is, people want him all the time and I have to be okay with that. I look down at the silverware and the beautiful crystal glasses, pretending not to notice.

"Welcome to the Lumiere, my name is Poppy and I will be your waitress today. I see that you have already chosen the tasting platter, which is an excellent choice, sir. Are there any particular drinks you would like to order, or can I offer my suggestion?"

"Yes, please, Poppy," I reply, even though she didn't ask me, because you know, there are two at this table. I look at the tasting platter on the menu and it is £285, and I nearly vomit in my mouth. You can get 40 Big Mac Meals from McDonald's for that.

Fuck my life. That's a lot of money.

"Great," she continues, still eye sexing Taron, "because there are a lot of different types of fish within a few of the dishes you have ordered, I would recommend a dry, crisp wine like a sauvignon blanc."

"That will be great, Poppy," I answer again, still getting no response from either Taron or our waitress.

"Great, I will get that sorted for you," she responds. She takes back our menu and disappears through the lights. Taron smiles at me with ease as if he hasn't realised what has happened, "I wasn't sure what you wanted, so I ordered the tasting menu."

He ordered for me? What would happen if I was allergic to shellfish?

I am annoyed that he didn't ask, but I don't say anything, instead, I do what I usually do, and simmer. The food is served quickly which I like as I am starving. The waitress wasn't wrong; there's a lot of fish, caviar, scallops, sardines, and lobster. Not one to ever turn down food, or try something new, I nibble on it all. The food is like an explosion of dreams in my mouth and whilst eating some of them, I cannot help but moan into my dinner; it is bloody fantastic, which sends some naughty looks from Taron. The only problem with it is that they are small portions, and I am a greedy girl, so by the time the cheese board comes out as our last course, I nearly cry because I am still hungry, and I don't want to be ungrateful, I can see that Taron has tried to make this night really special.

"Is there any food you didn't like?" he looks at me as he dabs his mouth with his £50 million napkin.

"All of it was delicious. I didn't get this way by being picky," I laugh, but he scowls at my comment and then brushes it away.

Well, I thought it was funny.

The air is thick with tension, but not sexual tension, the conversation has been awkward since we sat down for dinner, and a lot of his mannerisms have really pissed me off tonight.

Calm down, Daisy.

I feel I am getting myself in a right state when I should just relax and enjoy this.

"Tell me about you, Daisy. I don't know anything about you," he asks as he takes the last few sips of his wine.

I blow out a breath, "I have a sister whom you met. You know my father passed away and my mum is a deadbeat," I confess.

Wow, I can sum up my life in one sentence.

Taron studies me for a moment, "Have you travelled much?"

"I lived in Dubai for a bit when I was younger, I also went to Austria with Cole one Christmas. Oh, and I went to Ireland with my sister, her husband and his daughter so that he could show us his hometown." I summed the rest of my life up in two sentences.

I feel a bit pathetic.

I take a large gulp of wine so I would stop talking. I chance a peak at Taron, and his eyes are still on me, not wavering; his intense stare has me feeling unsettled.

"How's your week been?" Taron raises his eyebrows at my not-so-subtle change of subject, "I mean, I can't ask you about your past because, you know, so let's go with the obvious," he chokes on his wine a little and smirks.

"I'm really sorry again that you couldn't get in to see me play," he moves his hand across the table and takes mine in his. "It meant a lot to me that you tried to be there," he adds.

The whole thing was awful, Taron sent me some pretty shitty text messages, too, about how he felt that I had let him down by not being there. Once he finally answered his phone, the stubborn shit, and I explained what had happened, he seemed okay.

I roll my eyes a little, "Yeah, can't say the same, Taron; the media printed awful pictures of me crying. They are fucking relentless."

"Dirty mouth," he licks his lips and smirks, and I feel the heat rise in my cheeks, "It will get better. I'm sorry the media have slandered yours and my name," he looks down and sighs. My stomach rumbles and Taron chuckles from hearing my hunger pains.

"Shall we go and get some chips?" I think he feels sad that the portions were so small, too. My eyes light up as if he has read my mind. That was definitely not enough food for me.

You're mine - Taron

♥

ARCTIC MONKEYS — I WANNA BE YOURS

As we head out of the Dorchester Hotel, the cool breeze hits me in the face. I pull Daisy closer to me and link my fingers through hers, enjoying her warmth against mine. We set off at a steady pace up the road in search of a fast-food place.

"What do you love the most about being a paramedic?" I want to know everything about Daisy, I crave any information she gives me like a drug, a lifeline to this new life I am now set up to have.

"I like that every shift is different, that each patient is unique and I love solving the puzzle about what is wrong with someone. The clock is ticking when I see a new patient and sometimes, I only have moments to react before their life is in my hands. I want to save as many people as I can," her eyes are alight with passion, and I see that it is exactly how I feel when it comes to football. The passion on her face is one of the most beautiful expressions I have seen on her yet.

"As you saved me," she smiles and nods, "do you still believe it's the Nightingale syndrome?" she searches my face for a moment.

"I have no idea what this is. Sometimes, I think that it's best not to question it, as it makes my head hurt." I knew that feeling well. "What about you and football? Do you think you always wanted to be a footballer?" I can see she has expertly changed the subject, so I let the question drop for now.

"Yes, my gut, my whole body, my soul sings when I am out on the pitch. It feels like it is an extension of me when I am there - even if I am not playing, I feel whole." Daisy blows out a breath.

"Wow, that is something," she adds. I look at her, confused. "Your whole body and face just came alive when you spoke about it, I have not seen that in you before,"

"Or maybe it's just you, being near me," I press a small kiss to the side of her lips and lead her into the takeaway.

We order burgers and chips and eat them on the plastic seats in the stuffy takeaway. I think out of all of tonight's food, I like this best, only because I am not supposed to eat it on my diet. Daisy is practically singing to her food, and it makes me smile. I wipe the ketchup from her cheek. She smiles at me, but really, it's any excuse to touch her. It reminds me of when we went to Spain, and she had pasta sauce all over her face because the spaghetti was so long and...that's not a Daisy memory...that's a Melissa memory. Before I can process that, there's a bang against the window. I look up to see a small commotion outside, and I see that the press has found us.

"Shit," I mutter. Daisy follows my gaze, and her eyes nearly pop out of her head.

"Fuck...I can't do this, Taron, not again," she mutters. The press of late has really shaken her up, especially when she tried to come and see me at the football match, I was so angry with her. But the next day, when I read the awful crap the press printed about her, it was instantly forgiven. It really upsets me that the media have been so vindictive; I don't want another person in my life to suffer because of me. We needed to leave and fast! I suddenly have an idea from a movie I saw the other day. I go up to the counter.

"Hi, excuse me, sorry, I know this is not ideal, but can we escape through your fire exit?" the man looks confused, so I discreetly nod to the window where there is now a sizeable crowd.

"I thought I recognised you. You're the footballer. Can I have your autograph quickly? Then yes." I squiggle my name down on a few sheets of paper and gesture for Daisy to follow me. We walk into the kitchen and through the fire escape. Daisy then realises what's happening, and she starts to giggle.

"What?" I ask as we make a quick walk down the alley and back onto the main street. I look left and right and see they haven't cottoned on yet. Luckily, I made reservations at the Dorchester tonight, so it is a quick walk back.

"It's like one experience to the next with you, I don't know how you deal with it?" she declares.

"Neither do I, if I am honest. Come on, we can go back to the Dorch-ester, order a nightcap with room service and then I will call you a cab to take you home," I grab her hand, and we make a short walk back to the hotel with no more incidents.

I press the button to the top floor suite. I can't take my eyes off of her, and it seems she has the same problem as me. I want to bury myself so far inside Daisy that my mind takes on thoughts of its own. She licks her lips, and that's more than an invitation to press my lips to hers. It starts off slow and soft, but within moments, we have our hands all over one another and tongues everywhere. The ding of the lift indicates that we are on my floor. I reluctantly pull away whilst Daisy giggles again. I hold her hand in mine, leading her to my room. I slip in the key card and enter the room, closing the door and turning to her, " I won't presume Daisy-"

"Presume everything," she purrs and then her lips are on mine. My arm slips around her waist, pulling her closer, whilst my hand threads into her hair to get a deeper taste. I want to rip mine and her clothes off and fuck her senseless, but I can't; I need to do this right. Plus, in theory, isn't this my first time and holy shit, with that thought, I'm now nervous.

I guide her to the bedroom with my lips still on hers, pulling at her dress that I definitely can't get off whilst throwing my shoes and socks somewhere else. I push her down on the bed and stand over her.

"Daisy, you are so fucking beautiful, I don't even know what to do with you," I admit.

More like you don't know how to do this with her.

"Then let me help you. Strip!" she commands. Her words are like golden Viagra because I am ready to explode in my boxers. I start to sway my hips a little and take my tie off, throwing it at her; Daisy has the biggest grin on her face and is giggling. Her smiles make me relax, so I turn around and smack my arse, then wiggle out of my trousers; she's full-on laughing now. I slowly unbutton my shirt, swing it around and throw it on her as well. She stops giggling and then places her hands on my chest and softly runs her fingers through my chest hair; her hazel eyes swirl with desire.

"Jeez, Taron, you are so delicious with all this hair," she leans in and inhales my skin whilst softly stroking her fingertips up and down my chest, "you even smell amazing." That gentle movement makes me shudder. Her touching me like this is so erotic. I need her to stop touching me. Otherwise, this is going to end so badly for me. I don't want to be a man who is known to come too fast.

"Your turn," I huskily command. She looks up at me as I realise her face is very near my cock, and before I know what is happening, she pulls my boxers down, grabs my dick and puts her whole mouth over it. She is sucking, licking, and grabbing my balls – it's the most intense and sexual sensation I have ever felt. I put my hands on her shoulders to steady myself; my knees are weak and I am groaning like a mad man. "Daisy, if you carry on, I will blow my load in your mouth," and then I see the glint in her eye as if she has just accepted a silent challenge. Daisy is loving this, she then starts deep-throating me, and if I thought the licking and sucking were intense, then I am wrong. This is so far off the charts and is the most amazing thing I have ever felt. I couldn't stop myself, even if I tried, even if I were a professional, because Daisy is so magical with her mouth; I am coming down her throat, hard and heavy. I wonder for a moment if she might choke because if someone shoved their dick down my throat, I might vomit from the pressure. But as she sucks every last drop from me, she's all smiles with a dreamy expression on her face.

"Strip, damn it, woman," I demand. She gives me the salute and gets up from the bed. I capture a kiss from her lips and taste myself on her. She pushes me down onto the bed, and I look back at her in all her beautiful glory. She starts to undress, swaying and mimicking my movements slowly, and it makes me laugh at how comfortable we are with each other. She stands in front of me in her bright blue, lacy bra and knickers, and I blow out a breath of appreciation. My dick just woke up for round two because she is a sight, all curves and tits everywhere. Daisy is everything and more than I imagined her to be. As she stands before me, I pull her close to me, placing a small kiss on her stomach. She's perfection.

"You are mine, Daisy."

You are mine - Daisy

GESAFFELSTEIN & THE WEEKND – LOST IN THE FIRE

"You are mine, Daisy," his words are smooth and sexy and I am so turned on that I could probably slide across the bed sheets if I'm not careful. I've never been told I was anybody's before, not like this, and I like that feeling of being his, of being Taron's. His words shot straight to my heart. All those years, I have kept a solid wall around it, to protect myself from being hurt and scared and, in turn, never let anyone in, I started to crumble. "Get on the bed," he demands. I like being bossed about. Usually, it's me who takes control within the bedroom. I lie on the bed, and he hooks his fingers over my lacey knickers, and as he slowly pulls them down, he places short, gentle kisses up and down my legs. His lips kiss softly on the top of my mound; then he is licking and sucking. I take in a sharp breath as his stubble tickles and rubs against my inner thighs, sending lots of different sensations all over my body.

This is sexy, man stubble is a yes from me!

I am so excited he didn't need to go down on me. I was ready to fuck until I dropped, but I get it; I like the attention he gives me. With Taron taking his time on me, it will only make this so much more intense. I lay back and close my eyes, feeling the sensation of his tongue over me, he pushes a finger in and I groan, relishing anything he will give me. The funny thing is, although this is super sexy, oral sex for me has never got me off. I have never found it a turn-on, or an orgasmic point; the more I tried with previous partners, the more it became a moot point. No man has ever made me come through oral sex. I think my vagina is a bit broken when it comes to that sort of intimacy. But through sex, I can blow like a rocket from good hard fucking. I gave up my oral orgasming life a long time ago. Taron pushes another finger in whilst he nips and licks my sensitive area. The anticipation is growing.

"How close are you, Daisy?" I sit up slightly onto my elbows, looking down at him and jeez, I wish I could come all over his perfect face because who wouldn't want to? But this ain't happening. How do I say it without ruining the mood?

"I'm not one for oral sex," he raises his eyebrows at me and shrugs his shoulders, dismissing my comment as if he doesn't mind.

"Okay, I don't think it's for me anyway," is it for anyone? But people do it, because it makes the other one feel good. I feel slightly annoyed that he doesn't want to try harder to pleasure me. He wipes his mouth with the back of his hand, his eyes are now feral as he starts to climb over me.

Should I feel disappointed that he didn't try harder?

His eyes pierce mine and the thought and annoyance are soon forgotten as he kisses me, an all-consuming kiss, the one which is all tongue, lust and desire just before you have sex. These kisses are my favourite, the last build-up before the main course. I take off my bra because I want to feel all of him on me. As soon as I throw the bra off me, his lips are all over my boobs, grabbing them, swirling his tongue around my nipple. Now I like him touching these; if you went to town on my boobs, that's something I could get on board with. He nips on the tips and I gasp with delight; he looks up and gives me a cheeky smirk.

"Your tits are magical," he husks out. Tits, the only person I knew who called them tits was Stefan. I shudder and nearly vomit in my mouth thinking about that shit whilst I'm trying to fuck the most gorgeous man in England.

What the hell is wrong with me? Focus, Daisy!

I close my eyes again, taking a deep breath whilst he continues to flutter kisses along my chest and neck. Then his mouth is on mine again. I wrap my arms around his neck to bring him closer, feeling his erection against my stomach. This is really going to happen; no more dreaming or playing with myself thinking of him. He pulls away for a moment, I hear the crinkle as he opens the condom and pulls it over him. This bit, I find, is a bit of the lull, the pause before. Sometimes, I think it can be a mood killer.

"Are you ready?" Who's he asking, him or me? Because for this, I was born ready; I was ready the moment I gave him mouth-to-mouth on the pitch. He nudges at my entrance, "This is like a dream come true, Daisy," and then he pushes all the way in. I love this exact moment, the first contact; it is such an amazing feeling, and the fact that it's Taron is not lost on me. I am groaning like a dog on heat. Holy heck, he is big; my vagina is so ready to receive this gift that I have waited so patiently for - the gift of Taron's awesome and large dick.

His pace is slow at first, but I am not a slow person. I am fast and furious, and if you want to throw in a spank, I am all for that, too. I find direction is key to my pleasure, and I am all for the pleasure.

"Taron," he looks at me, lost in the sensation, "I am not going to break, you know?" I give him a smile and urge him on, deeper, faster. I wiggle my hips and then he takes the hint and is right there with me. He picks up the speed, and his lips are on mine again. I deepen the kiss, pushing my tongue inside him as he groans.

I need more of him.

I roll him over and then get on my hands and knees, wanting him to take me from behind. He's in me within seconds, hard and fast and he's hitting all the right spots. He moves his hands around and starts to caress my breast, flicking and rubbing them with the tips of his fingers, and that's it to push me over the edge. I shudder and moan, feeling the orgasm build and explode whilst I clench around him. I hear a guttural moan from

Taron and feel him pulsing inside me in the last deep thrusts, and then he stills, leaning his head on my back. "Fuck Daisy, I might have another heart attack at this rate."

I giggle as he pulls out, disposing of the condom. He kisses me gently on the lips. "I'm going to take a shower," he goes into the bathroom and shuts the door. I wait for a moment, expecting him to come back out and invite me in. I hear the shower turn on, and then nothing.

Oh. I guess he didn't want me to join.

I shouldn't feel hurt that he didn't want to hold me for a moment after sex, talk, or even ask me to join him for round two in the shower, not even a soap down, right? What an odd feeling that I want more for once, yet it is not given. I feel a bit embarrassed and annoyed that I have let myself feel this way. I shake away the thought because when he finishes his shower and joins me back in bed, maybe that will be round two then.

There are a lot of thoughts floating around my head as I lie in the rather large king-size bed, with its heavenly soft sheets lulling me into a deep sleep. I have had a really busy week with shifts, and post-orgasms always make me feel dozy. I fall asleep before Taron climbs back into bed.

The morning after - Taron

THE NEIGHBOURHOOD - DADDY ISSUES

My phone buzzes next to my bedside table, and I roll over, happy to have finally had sex with Daisy. But when I open my eyes, she is gone. A pang of sadness hits me, and I feel hurt that she left before I woke up. Was it that bad? Was I that bad? Did this mean she didn't want to be with me? I didn't know how to be in a relationship, I didn't know what or how to do this, I don't remember. I look through my phone quickly and see that she has texted.

Had to leave early, as Kevin was on his own and didn't want to wake you up. You looked so peaceful. X

My phone buzzes again and I can see that it's my personal trainer/physio/rehab person. I check the time and see that I am late for an appointment. "Shit," I mutter. I fire off a text and ask him to meet me at the hotel gym instead, and I will compensate him for his time. I have never overslept.

That's what a good sex session does to you, apparently.

I pull on my joggers and t-shirt with a smile. If that was sex the first time, imagine a whole day of it filled with Daisy, just that thought alone made my cock rock solid. If she had been here still, we could have sorted this out by fucking like rabbits, but she went home to her dog.

I hate dogs.

Next time we do this, I will make sure there is a dog sitter. I'm sure I can ask my assistant to walk her bloody dog. Then I can have Daisy to myself all day and all night, taking my time with her because having sex once with her curvy body is definitely not enough for me. I don't think it will ever be enough when it comes to Daisy. I send her a text back;

I missed you when I woke up. When can I see you again?

I hope she says today, as I only have a few more weeks until I am signed off fully. Then my training and schedule will get more intense, and I won't be able to see Daisy as much. Her schedule at the hospital is insane already. We would really have to plan our days in. Daisy is exceptional; she has me guessing all the time about what she wants, and I like that mystery about her. I thought all women wanted to be treated with fancy dinners, fancy wine and flowers (that's what the guys on my team said), but it seems that Daisy is not just any woman, and I am learning that fast.

The training session went well with PS training, I am able to do all the stretches, fitness goals and routines set today, which is the first time. I am so pleased and proud of my recovery; nobody wants to be ill or unwell, but when you are handed what I was given, you work with what you have got, and I have done just that. I've embraced it.

After training, I order room service of some healthy, non-fat, low-sugar dinner which tastes like air and oddly like porridge - my trainer told me off about eating burgers. Still, for Daisy, I would eat them just to be able to look at her face and hear her sounds as she bites into one. That memory from last night alone is going to be for a lot of wanking in the future. I shower and change into some casual clothes, deciding that I want to surprise Daisy at her place. I want to see her. I know she is off today, and I am bubbling with so much excitement in wanting to be near her again. Plus, more sex would just be the icing on the cake.

I call my driver and head down to reception. I loiter there until my driver arrives. I see that the media has gotten wind of where I am staying, so I make a mental note to ring my assistant in the car to get her to move my hotel. I knew it wouldn't be long until they all found me, but two weeks wasn't that bad – plus, if Daisy is going to stay more, then I need to keep them away for as long as possible so that they wouldn't scare her off. I mean, they still scare me a bit.

The drive over to her place is long, with stupid traffic jams and roadworks. The driver is complaining because they only dug up this part of the road a few weeks ago, and now they are doing it again for gas works. I think about texting Daisy to say that I am coming, but I want to surprise her. On the way, I purchase some very expensive-looking chocolate. I almost convince myself to order her a burger instead, but my driver reassures me that chocolates will be a better idea.

I get the driver to park by the fire exit, I wait as he walks around the front of the apartment, into the building and comes and lets me in. The media are here, too, but I don't want them to have a field day over my arrival when I am trying to establish a relationship with Daisy. I decide to take the stairs; she's only two floors up. I do this slowly, taking deep breaths. When I get to the top, it's like another personal win. I'm not out of breath, and I'm not feeling light-headed.

Today is a fantastic day.

I knock on the door with such pep that I smile to myself. The dog barks, and I inwardly groan. When Daisy opens the door, her face falls, "Taron," she squeaks, "I didn't know you were coming over; you didn't say." I smile at her because we had sex, and I want to do it again, right now! Just being near her makes me so happy. Her hair is in a messy bun, she has no make-up on, she's wearing leggings and a baggy t-shirt, and she looks beautiful.

"I thought I would surprise you," I give her a quick kiss on the lips and pass her the chocolate.

She smiles, "Thank you...you know you don't need to get me gifts every time we see each other?"

"Who's that?" another man's voice calls from within her apartment. Her smile is replaced with a frown, and I've gone from being happy to really angry within seconds. Daisy sighs and opens the door wide for me to come in. I walk into her apartment, and there sitting on the sofa is some chump.

"Taron, this is Daniel. Daniel, Taron," I narrow my eyes at him. The dog comes trotting over, I quickly pat him on the head; he takes a sniff at me and then walks away.

"I know who you are," Daniel responds with an easy smile. He stands up and walks over to me, hand out, ready for me to shake. I look at him, his hand and then back up at him.

"I don't know who you are," I respond. Daisy sighs at my remark.

"I work with Daisy at the hospital," he seems to get the hint that I am not shaking his hand, but his smile is still there.

"Is that right?" I add.

"So, it's true then, the two of you?" he gestures towards Daisy and then me.

"What's true?" I ask, not sure where this conversation is going, but I don't care; this shithead needs to leave.

"That you're fucking?" he declares.

"Daniel!" Daisy cries.

"What? You suddenly stop calling, I read what's in the news; I wanted to see for myself. So, it's true then; you left your wife for Daisy." He blows out a breath and shakes his head as if I have made a mistake. I step closer to Daniel, I don't care if he's the same height and build as me; if I need to punch him, I won't hesitate. He levels with me; he's not scared of me, but that makes two of us. No one insults Daisy or Melissa.

"Get out," I growl. He chuckles.

"I'm going," he puts his hands up in surrender, grabbing his jacket as he steps around me towards the door. As he walks past Daisy, he mutters, "You could do so much better." Daisy's eyes are trained on me, and I know she can see red. I stalk towards him, open the door and push him through it, slamming the door in his face. I hear laughter from behind the door, and his footsteps echo away. My heart is beating wildly, I feel my body vibrating with anger, and I take deep breaths to calm my breathing. It turns out I'm jealous, too. After a few moments, I look at Daisy; she has her hands on her hips and her eyebrows arched.

She's mad at you, Taron.

"Taron, you can't come barging in here-" but as she is starting her verbal assault, I stalk towards her and smash my lips onto hers. I am jealous, angry, insulted, turned on and raging with desire. I pull hard on her hair and curl my tongue into hers; she resists only slightly until she opens up, moaning into my mouth. I walk her slowly backwards until she comes in contact with the wall, and I am pulling her and my clothes off with such a manic speed that I am not surprised we are both naked so quickly. I try to calm my mind and place a softer trail of kisses down her neck, collarbone, breasts, and stomach. Then I grab a condom from the pocket of my discarded trousers on the floor beside us and kiss my way back up her body, nipping and biting her but also spending a little more time on her fantastic tits. I cover myself quickly and don't even ask if she is ready because I need to fuck this rage out. I push in deep and hard, and she cries out with joy, threading her fingers through my hair and guiding my mouth back to hers. I pace myself deep and hard; each thrust eases my anger and jealousy. I almost want to make her feel the pain I did when I saw shithead here. But there's something wild in Daisy's eyes (when I come up for air). That look alone urges me to push harder and faster, it turns me on more. Her moans spur me into a frenzy and within moments, I feel her clenching around me, and I am seeing stars as I shoot my load into her because fuck me, she feels so warm and perfect when I am inside her. I still for a moment and then kiss her softly on the lips, feeling the release and the calm.

"I'm still mad at you," she murmurs over my kisses.

"Yeah, well, I'm mad at you. You should never be alone with a man like that in your apartment unless you want to be fucked by him. I'm the only man that should be allowed in this apartment with you, alone, like this. Do you understand?"

The morning after -
Daisy

CHASE ATLANTIC - FRIENDS

I left Taron early the next morning. After we'd had sex (and me a cheeky nap), I debate whether to stay, but I decide that it would be best to go home. I couldn't get comfortable, not like my own bed and I had a lot of emotions going through my head, so the only place I knew I would sleep would be my own bed. Plus, Kevin had been on his own most of the evening and as much as I would have liked round two, I was unsure how to face Taron in the morning.

All these new emotions and feelings for him are making me so confused. I feel so differently towards Taron than I have to any other man I have met before. I have never wanted to be in a relationship or even entertained the thought properly until now. Even though the sex had been great, it really was, but somewhere in the back of my mind, I am slightly disappointed the sex wasn't more. It's like I have worked myself up about him. I had put him on this pedestal that he could never reach the standards that I had him at.

Damn imagination.

It's like when people say how amazing a new film is, I invest in the hype and hear reviews of it. Yet when I finally get to see it, I watch the film, and after it finishes, I think it's just 'okay.' Stupid social media and friends, I bought into how brilliant the film is supposed to be, and it wasn't amazing. I leave the cinema feeling disappointed in the movie, even though it's good enough. Is this the same thing with Taron?

Fuck, is Taron a disappointing sexual partner?

No, that can't be it. Maybe the first time is like a warm-up to the most amazing orgasms I am going to face in my life, and now that the first time is out of the way, it will be onwards and upwards. The problem is that I expected fireworks, and instead, I got a little sizzle.

Why am I trying to pep talk myself? I am trying too hard.

After I slipped out of the hotel room and grabbed a taxi home, I texted Taron to let him know I had left because if I woke up, I would be annoyed if he had left without saying goodbye. I took Kevin on a huge walk. I walked for hours, thinking about my feelings. Dad, Taron, do I even admit to myself that I thought of Stefan?

I think one of the reasons why I 'don't do feelings' is because my first true feelings were for Stefan. Stefan hurt me so much with my young, impressionable 16-year-old self. Despite everything, I still hate him now. I'm not sure that feeling will ever go away, but at the time, I thought I was in love, true love, with him. I was so wrong, so far from the truth, that I didn't know if I could ever trust my feelings like that with other people again.

Until Taron.

So, in the past, when I started to get those feelings again, it brought back the pain, the hurt, and the shame, and I couldn't cope. I run as far away from those feelings as I can because I hate those feelings. But now it is time to grow up, I can't keep running away. Yes, I know Stefan was a shit, but it's in the past. He can't hurt me anymore. Yes, Dad died, and that hurt will never go away, but by closing my feelings off, I am only hurting and stopping myself from actually being with someone who could make me happy.

Could Taron make me happy?

It's a morning of revelations and by the time I get back to my apartment, I am feeling lighter and more refreshed. I almost go in the front way, forgetting the fucking press are STILL camped outside my apartment building. I slip through the fire exit and walk up the stairs slowly, as I know how much Kevin hates going up the stairs. I check my phone to see that a text from Cora has come through asking if I am okay – I will deal with that one later and one from Taron, saying he misses me, and that makes me smile.

I have to try. I have to see where this will go because just that text had my whole body vibrating with excitement, with tiny butterflies taking flight in my tummy. I like this feeling. As I approach my door, lost in thought, I see that Daniel is waiting in the hallway. I stop, confused.

"What are you doing here?"

"I came to see you," he flirts, throwing me his best smile. I know that in the past, that would be enough to get me naked and some very good sex. But now, there is nothing between us because the relationship we had was fucking only; there was no emotion involved, no connection. In fact, he did small things that really irritated me. Yes, he was great with his dick, and his face was beautiful, but there was nothing going on underneath. We have nothing in common, and he hates Kevin.

So does Taron—Shhh brain.

"Has something happened at the hospital?" I ask innocently.

"Let me in, Daisy, let's talk," he smiles. Kevin gives him a sniff and doesn't even bother to ask for a stroke; he knows the drill.

The dog hater!

Dogs have some sixth sense about dog lovers, and Daniel was definitely not one of them. I unlock the door, and he follows me through. I unclip Kevin, who bounds off for a drink and a lie-down. I shut the door, pop the kettle on, take off my jacket and busy myself, unsure what Daniel is doing here or what he wants.

It makes me feel a little nervous.

"Cuppa?" He smiles, nods, takes his jacket off, and then sits on the sofa. "Make yourself at home," I mumble. I make the drinks and hand him his, sitting at the far end of the sofa. I didn't want him to get the wrong impression.

"Why have you not been answering my texts?" he asks. I take a sip of my tea, surprised at his question. I silently cursed myself that I hadn't waited a moment. The burning liquid is now sliding down my oesophagus as my body protested the heat and will probably burn every damn internal organ now! I know I am going to have the furry tongue feeling for the next few days. I sigh.

"You text me for a hookup, I said I didn't want to do that anymore." He puts his tea on the coffee table and shuffles towards me, taking my hand in his. His unwanted touch takes me by surprise.

"I've done a lot of thinking, Daisy, and I really like you, so if this is because you want something more, then I am here to tell you that I am ready."

"You're ready?" He nods, and I frown, unsure where this declaration has come from. We never said we wanted to date each other. It was friends with benefits if that's what you wanted to call it. I wonder if we are even friends; maybe 'acquaintances with benefits' is a better fit. He smiles widely at me, waiting for my answer as if this is what I have wanted all along. I never gave out the signals that I wanted more, and I think back through our time together, and he didn't either. "No, no, that isn't what I want, Daniel," his face falls for a moment, "I ended it because I didn't want to carry on this arrangement anymore."

"Because you want more?" he asks.

"No," I reply honestly. I really did think we were on the same page about this.

"No?"

"Not with you. Don't get me wrong, what we had was fun when it was happening, but we both agreed, did we not? Nothing more, just casual sex." He looks at me for a moment, leans forward, and kisses me. The kiss is sloppy and brief; I push him back and stand up.

"What do you think you're doing?" I demand.

"I thought maybe you needed a reminder," he picks up his tea and sips it, assessing the situation. I'm simmering with rage now; I didn't want him to kiss me and this whole conversation is shooting off a bad feeling into my stomach. He needs to leave.

I cross my arms at him, trying to hide the fact that I am now shaking, "I don't need a reminder, Daniel; I am capable of making my own decisions. My decision is no-"

A knock on the door stops the conversation from going any further and I'm relieved of the distraction. I need to get Daniel out of my apartment now. However, when I answer the door and see Taron in all his Greek godliness, I nearly die inside because I have no idea how I am going to explain this. Taron smiles and passes me some very expensive-looking chocolate. Why does he keep buying me stuff?

Maybe he wants to buy my time like a prostitute?

The thought is squashed almost immediately when Daniel opens his big, fat mouth. Now Taron knows there's another male in my apartment. He is all fluffed up like a peacock and asserting his dominance towards Daniel. It's a little sexy yet really fucking embarrassing. He can't come into my house and be this person.

Do I even know who he is anyway?

When he slams the door in Daniel's face, I feel only relief that Daniel is out of my apartment, but I am so bloody angry at Taron. How dare he come into my apartment like he owns the place and me? Before I can even protest properly, his mouth is on mine, and we are undressing each other because, apparently, I am really into angry, frantic sex. The lust in his eyes is enough to make me into a puddle, but the sex is hungry, fast, and deep. It's absolutely fantastic. I am coming within minutes on his dick, and oh my jeez, it is so good. It was so different to last night and, thankfully, much better.

I am so relieved because no matter how much I tried to say it was okay, sex is so important to me, and when I felt yesterday could have been better, I questioned everything. But this, this right here against the wall, is amazing and everything I thought sex with Taron would be.

"I'm still mad at you," I murmur over his kisses. I feel so happy and content from my orgasm that my words of anger don't really sound convincing. I'm not really angry with him anymore if this is how I feel after he fucks me.

"Yeah, well, I am mad at you. You should never be alone with a man like that in your apartment unless you want to be fucked by him. I am the only man that should be allowed in this apartment with you, alone, like this, do you understand?" he glowers.

I sigh as he pulls out and starts dressing himself. I grab my clothes and put them back on, unsure of what to say. I don't want to fall out with him about it, but I don't know how to deal with him being this jealous.

Don't mention the kiss.

"Look, Daisy, I don't know how to date or do any of this relationship stuff, but you make me crazy. It's crap that I can't remember my life, but I am serious when I say you are mine, nobody else's. So that means not being alone with men like Daniel, just me." He pulls me close, kissing me softly on the lips, and looks into my eyes. "Let's order takeout and watch one of those ridiculous old-school films you've been going on about."

I should feel happy that Taron chose me, that Taron wants to be with me, but it doesn't quite come. I am unsure if my brain hasn't caught on to the fact that I have made the decision to try a relationship with Taron, and it wanted to run away again, or if something isn't quite right. I brush away those feelings and settle in on the sofa, cuddling up to Taron and watching some timely classics.

Sister time - Daisy

ALEC BENJAMIN – IF WE HAVE EACH OTHER

The following week passes in a blur with horrible shift work, the media being their usual in-my-face self, and a lot of sex with Taron. The sex is getting better; we are exploring what each other's likes are, but it seems that the angry sex was when he really came alive, but that dirty man hasn't come out to play again and I'm a little disappointed. I really did want it all with Taron. Is sex really that important if it isn't electric and all-consuming all of the time? Is it where we skip over that bit and go to what most married couples get to five or ten years down the line in their relationship - where sex is still great but not the fireworks that it once was?

Do I really need the fireworks when everything else with us seems to fit?

I head over to Cora and Zach's house for tea; she's made lasagna - I love her lasagna; it reminds me of Dad's. They've filled me in on every minute of their holiday; even Amy seems chipper and excitable at the dinner table. I've brought Kevin; he loves being here, the treats and the extra attention he gets; he probably thinks he's on dog holiday.

"No phones at the table, Amy," Zach says as he takes the last bite of his dinner. She groans and puts it back on the shelf behind her.

"The last place we stayed at," Cora continues, "was amazing; we were in this hotel right by the lakes. We could roll out of bed and swim in it and the food was insane." I love it when my sister is excited as she is so animated. "I ate my weight in pizza," she beamed. The clatter of the plates alerts Kevin that food time for humans is now over, and maybe he can beg for scraps. Not that he needs to, as I see Amy is already feeding him under the table and scratching behind his ear.

"I want a dog, please. Can we get one?" Amy whines.

Zach laughs, "I think that is something we need to discuss together, but not right this minute," he collects the plates from the table whilst Amy huffs. I polish off my wine and I'm glad that they are back. I've missed our weekly dinners and family chats. Looking at the last few pictures on Cora's phone from their honeymoon and it really did look amazing. She's practically beaming in every photo. Zach puts the plates in the sink, comes back to the table and drinks the last of his beer. "I tell you what, Amy? Let's take Kevin for a walk whilst Cora and Daisy catch up," just the word 'walk' and Kevin is up and bouncing around. He's running to the other side of the kitchen, sticks his nose in the dog bag and gets his lead. Honestly, I swear the dog gets more human every day. Amy seems appeased by this and gets her shoes and jacket, grabs her phone from the shelf and quickly takes a selfie with the dog. Kevin is living his best life.

"Thanks, Zach," I say as he kisses Cora on the head, gives me a goofy smile and follows Amy out of the door. We wash the dishes as I fill her in on the press, Taron, the way I have been feeling, even the sex because I desperately need to talk to someone about this. To say it out loud, to rationalise my new crazy life. But, as much as I love my sister, she can't lie for shit; she doesn't look happy.

"What?" I ask.

"I'm worried, Daisy. I want you to let someone in; I'm all for you actually getting into a relationship, but this one," she sighs, knowing whatever she says next will piss me off, "it doesn't feel right; the whole media thing scares me... I saw what it did to Sophie. I know, I know, swear at me all you like, but if I don't say anything, Daisy, it will eat away at me, and I just want you to be happy and not get hurt."

"Fucking hell," I mutter

"What?" she asks with surprise.

"You sound like Cole," I say, wiping the last dish dry, putting it in the cupboard and then sitting back at the dinner table. She blows out a breath.

"He has spoken to you about this?" she asks.

I nod, "When I took him to the airport a few weeks back," she joins me at the table and holds my hand.

"I love you, Daisy, and I will support you no matter what. If he's your one, then it is what it is, but I don't know. I can't put my finger on it; something isn't sitting right." I burst into tears; I can't help it; he has me feeling every fucking emotion. The emotions I think I forgot to feel about boys in my teenage years, and I can't stand it. Cora envelops me in the biggest hug.

"Oh, don't cry; I'm sorry, I didn't mean to upset you. Plus, shite, you are crying. Is everything okay? You never cry."

I don't know if I am okay. I am so ridiculously happy, scared, and miserable in one go that I think I might be having a mid-life crisis or early menopause. I definitely wasn't okay.

"Another joy of being with Taron," I admit.

"You're not pregnant, are you?" she joked.

"God, no, definitely not," I declare.

"I am," I gasp, pull back and look at my sister, who now has tears streaming down her face.

"What? This is a good thing, right?" I bleat.

"Yes, of course, it is great. My period is like six weeks late. I thought it was the stress of the wedding and shite with that, but it seems not. I just didn't plan on getting pregnant so soon. I've got the tour with the orchestra next month; I am going to be horribly pregnant, and I don't even know how I am going to do this; we hadn't discussed even trying."

"What has Zach said?" I ask, handing her a tissue.

She then starts to full-on cry, "I haven't told him yet," she whines.

"Ah fuck," I mutter.

"And I drank at the wedding," she cries.

"Yeah, but not loads; I'm sure it's fine," I soothe my sister.

"I know, but I drank, and I drank on holiday, and what if I have killed the baby before I even become the baby's mother," she now has started to howl.

Jeez!

"You are not making sense. Look, just book yourself into a scan; you can do it privately and go and reassure yourself."

"I even ate soft cheese," she continues, ignoring everything I'm saying to calm her down, "I'm a bad mother already; I'm turning into our mum without even realising it."

"Cora, bloody hell sister, I am going to slap you in a minute if you don't shut up," I grab her by the shoulders and shake her a little, "you are nothing like mum, you never will be, look how well you have cared for me, and Amy, you are an excellent mother already."

She takes a deep breath and sniffs, giving me a small smile with her mascara-stained eyes, "Really?" I wipe her eyes carefully with another tissue and smooth her hair, nodding.

"Really and-" The door slams, and Zach appears.

"I forgot poo bags and-" he stops in the doorway, looking at us both. He narrows his eyes, assessing the situation, "What the shit is going on?" he demands.

"I'm pregnant," she blurts out, "Surprise!" she laughs, not a normal Cora laugh, but a manic one.

Okay, not exactly how I thought she was going to tell him, but you know that will do! He looks at her, not saying anything, and I literally want to back out of the room, being in their intimate moment.

Why isn't he saying anything? Oh, jeez, did he not want any more children? Cora said they hadn't discussed it.

Then the biggest smile covers his face and his eyes are all wide, "Are you serious?" He rounds the table and she nods, returning him with a very relieved smile on her face. He lifts her out of the chair, squashing her with the biggest hug, and showers her with kisses. Then they kiss manically and with such desire. Now, I am definitely encroaching on their intimate moment. I get up and quietly walk over to Kevin's stuff, grabbing the poo bags.

"I will go with Amy and Kevin for a walk," I call as I am heading out the door.

Yeah, they totally didn't hear me.

Football life - Taron

PANIC! AT THE DISCO - READY TO GO

I will officially be signed off with a clean bill of health in 13 days, I can't fucking wait.

Proper training starts in 16 days and if I pass all the tests, I can start training with my team again. Well, not full-on training, but I have already drafted up a phased training schedule and spent hours poring over it with my manager, too. He hopes that around halfway through the season, I can be back on the pitch. The manager wants it to be half the game, but we will take that week by week and under the advice of my doctor, too. He thinks I should be okay to be a substitute for the last 5 minutes or so of some games - sadly, not the first few games; he really wants to see me back to my full glory and I am stoked. My doctor still moans at me constantly; he thinks that getting back to my fittest could take anywhere between six months to a year. I don't know if I can wait that long. Regardless, they all seem really positive and on board. The team have been so supportive in my recovery. A few teammates have been coming to the hotel the last few weeks, every morning for either a training session or a cycle around the park, talking to me about strategies, the games, other players, them as people and me. They are the best team I could ask for; everyone is amazing, and I feel so lucky to have this strong support network around me.

I now know all their names; we've also made it a thing that after our meetings, we sit and watch previous games with other teams that we are playing this season, looking at their strikers, defence, their tactics and weaknesses. I love, live and breathe football, and I go to bed every night with a smile on my face.

I love the fans, too; they're everywhere, giving me stuff, saying how great I am, wanting pictures and autographs. I really do like the attention from the fans. It makes me feel good about myself, important even. It makes me want to work harder to get better. My trainer has given me a daily schedule with 100 reps of different exercises for my arms, legs, and abs. But I am making sure I have been doing 150, even 200 reps, pushing myself a little bit more, and I tell the fans about everything I have been doing. They hang on to every word I say. I don't want to let them down.

I love the fans.

My phone buzzes, waking me from a nap I didn't know I needed. The headaches have been terrible the last few days. I rang the doctor, and they upped my medication, but it doesn't seem to be helping. It makes me dozy and sleepy. I don't want to sleep more. I told my doctor this, but he says I am overdoing it, and that is why I am so tired. My body tells me I am not overdoing it; my head doesn't seem to listen to anything anyway.

I went for a brain scan last week to start my new cognitive therapy. It was four days away, with an intense treatment plan, which, from their results with previous patients, have helped unlock memories in only a few weeks. It focused on my breathing, memory, recall, sight, balance and stimulation of my system, which was definitely an overwhelming sensory experience. The therapy helps to promote more blood flow and neurons into my brain, whatever that means. Then, to top it off, I had very in-depth and odd conversations with my new therapist. I think these sessions have set off my headaches into something else.

I look at my phone, and I am surprised that Melissa has texted with:

We need to talk.

We haven't spoken in weeks. I have rung her and texted her a bunch of times, but she has avoided my calls at all costs. To be honest, it pissed me off. If she claims to be so in love with me, why won't she even speak to me? It doesn't make sense, and now, all of a sudden, she wants to talk and thinks I will just fawn over her. She can piss right off. I will answer that later and let her sweat it out for a while.

My phone rings, disturbing my thoughts; it's my press officer. I groan; she hates me. I'm half tempted to send her call to voicemail, but she's very persistent and will continue to call me or even turn up at my door.

"Hey," I say.

"Taron, this one isn't good. I have tried damage control as much as possible, but it's going to print tomorrow," she declares.

"What is?" I bark out.

"Daniel Kirby, heard of him?"

"The doctor that works with Daisy?" I ask, confused.

"Yep, that's the one; he's sold his story about you and her to the paper; he's even accusing you of hitting him in a fury of rage. Did this happen?"

"No, I didn't hit him. I pushed him out the door for insulting me," I declare.

"Why didn't you tell me that happened?" She's angry now and I can hear her muttering under her breath.

"Because he's a prick, and I didn't think he would sell his crappy story to the paper," I boom.

"He has, and it's bad," she points out, her voice hard and stony.

"Bad, how?"

"He's saying that Daisy is in love with him; they kissed and you are jealous. That you are having this affair with her to get back at him and your wife, some shit about drinking and drugs, but that won't fly. You have a clean record; with that. He's basically calling you a worthless cheater, that you had this thing with Daisy before your incident, and that you are faking the memory loss."

She doesn't mince her words and says it exactly how it is.

"Fucking shithead, find his address, find his address now! I am going to go over there and I'm going to kill him!" I shout at her down the phone. She sighs and waits to respond when my breathing is a bit more under control.

"Taron, don't be so reckless; you need to think about this rationally with a comeback; the press will be all over this today, the latest tomorrow morning. You need a statement to be released. You need to be put in front of the camera and tell them that it's all lies. I am putting something together as we speak, but the sooner we release this, the better it will be. I will call you again in a few hours," she hangs up, clearly not interested in my outburst or what I have to say.

I slam the phone against the wall; what the fuck is wrong with people? I needed to find this little shit and put him in his place once and for all. I check the time, fucking hell, Daisy will be here in a minute. I need to warn her that the press might be downstairs. I ring her, but it goes straight to voice mail; I ring again, I text, but does she ring me back?

Nope.

Shit.

I think I'm falling -
Daisy

OLIVIA RODRIGO – 1 STEP FORWARD, 3 STEPS BACK

I'm on my way over to see Taron, I am buzzing with excitement. I haven't seen him in person for several days due to my night shifts, his training and, more importantly, his therapy. I wondered if he had gained any more of his memories back. Taron has been so obsessed with getting signed off in a few weeks that he's been pushing himself even more than usual. But I get it; football is everything to him. I have asked my neighbour to look after Kevin so that I can spend the actual night with Taron and not have to shoot off for work or Taron to his training sessions. We will spend the night and the whole day together.

He can be witness to my morning breath and bedhead, the works. My butterflies are flying rapidly around my stomach. It's beyond ridiculous.

Taron sends his driver over to pick me up, which makes me laugh. This sort of money at his fingertips is only what I have imagined in my dreams when I win the lottery – a great fantasy. However, I was slightly disappointed when I got in the car that he wasn't there. But I'm already armed and at the ready. My hair is straightened, everything shaved and underneath my dress is the sexiest lingerie that I own. My phone buzzes, pulling me out of some very dirty thoughts, and it's Cora.

"Hey, sister," she coos over the phone.

"Hey, how's it going?" I know why she's ringing and I'm practically bouncing on my seat, the driver gives me an odd look, but he doesn't say anything.

"We went for the scan and it's all fine; there's a baby in there with a heartbeat and everything, 11 weeks five days, wait a minute, let me send it to you," my phone buzzes and I open up the grey, fuzzy scan picture and my heart melts. I have no bloody clue what I am looking at, but it's my sister's baby and I could not be any prouder. Since Cora confessed her pregnancy to Zach, they have been loving life. Cole cried when we rang him; in fact, it was a whole lot of tears. Amy cried and screamed with excitement as she said she'd always wanted a brother or a sister and then said she was definitely not changing any dirty nappies because, as she worded it, 'so gross'.

"I'm so happy for you guys," I laugh; happily, I see a text come through from Taron but swipe it away. I will see him in a few minutes anyway; he can wait.

"I rang Trinity, and she's so happy, and Adam," she sighs, "is still not taking my calls; I don't get it, radio silence. I asked Trinity if he's changed his number or has gone on holiday, but she says she's not heard from him much either, but he's answering her texts; I don't get it. I'm worried. Maybe I should go round and see him. Did he seem okay with you at the wedding?"

Is this where I reveal the truth or leave it be? I remember that Adam told me not to say anything to Cora, and as much as I love my sister, she's already on a wobble about the baby, and I think this will only hurt her further. Plus, if he wants to talk to her about it, he can do it himself; this ain't my fight. He's had several years to get this feeling off his chest and did nothing about it, so he can sort that out when he is ready. Also, I already have enough on my plate as it is.

"No, nothing that springs to mind," I hope she can't tell I am lying, but my mind wanders away as we start to pull up to the hotel Taron is staying in. It's absolutely swarming with the press, "What the hell?" I murmur.

"What? What's going on?" my sister calls from the phone.

"The press is here like someone famous has died," I say, counting at least 20 reporters.

"Oh shite, not again; what happened? What did you do, Daisy?" her voice stern.

"Me? I haven't done anything," I look to the driver for answers, but he shrugs; he doesn't seem to know what's going on either.

"I will drive round the back," he calls.

"I gotta go, Cora; I will call you later." I hang up and read the text from Taron;

Pick up the phone, do not go in the front.

I ring Taron; he picks up on the first ring.

"Damn, Daisy, why do you never answer your phone?" he sounds pissed off and angry and that gets me all sorts of excited.

That is not a normal response.

"What's happened?" I ask.

"Your so-called prick of a friend sold you out!" he shouts.

"We are heading round the back," I tell him. I have no idea what friend he is talking about or what story has leaked to the press, but it doesn't sound good, and I inwardly groan because another round with the press is something I don't want to face.

"Right, I will meet you there, but they're everywhere." We pull up at the back entrance, and yes, they are here too, but not as many. The driver ushers me out and I feel like I might just drown in it. Everyone is shouting at me again; my heart rate picks up and I feel my clammy hands. They're so loud, pushing and pulling, even calling me names. I hear Daniel's name being shouted and how can I live with myself?

What does Daniel have to do with this?

My stomach sinks and starts to form knots. I push my way through the crowd whilst the driver ushers them out of the way. Then Taron is there with a full-on glare, and his eyes are full of rage. He literally pulls me into the hotel door.

"Sod off!" he shouts.

"Is that an official statement?" someone shouts back. I'm practically running to keep up with Taron's angry walk, his hand firmly in mine; he doesn't let go. He's practically vibrating with anger. He hits the call button on the lift so hard that I think he may have broken it. We walk into the lift and go up in silence. Taron isn't even looking at me; he's looking at the ceiling as if saying a silent prayer. The lift dings, and he drops my hand, storming out of it through to the hallway, not his usual soft kisses or touching me at any opportunity. I feel like a naughty child, and blaming me for something I have no idea about.

He opens the room with the keycard; I walk in silently after him, unsure how to channel this side of Taron. He's simmering with rage and pacing the hotel room. I put my bags by the door in case he doesn't want me to stay and watch him carefully for a few minutes. I know he won't hurt me, but I don't want to upset him further. The knot in my stomach has formed into sadness. He then looks at me and stalks towards me, and his lips are on mine; his kisses are so frantic and passionate and all-consuming, his tongue is deep, and his hands are in my hair.

"You are a very naughty girl," he moans, smacking me on the bum hard. I yelp with surprise and he gives me a wicked smile. His lips are back on mine, but he's being too rough and bites my lip. I pull away from him.

"Taron, that hurt," I admit. "I know you are angry-"

"I'm not angry," he interrupts; he holds my chin in place firmly, "I am furious." He then strokes the hair out of my face and then traces his fingertips across my cheeks. His dark eyes soften a little and then his kisses are a little more careful. He leads me to the sofa and takes off my dress. His eyes work their way down and up again, enjoying my lingerie display as he licks his lips in desire. "Daisy, you look amazing," he kisses my neck, then grabs my boobs over my lingerie, pushing his face into them whilst nipping, licking and kissing them, which makes me giggle. "You should wear this all the time. Turn around." I do as he says, "I don't even need to undress you; you've come all packaged for me like a present," I hear his zipper go and the crinkle of the condom; he smacks my bum again and I yelp; he puts pressure on my back so I bend over the sofa and he swipes a finger over my mound, "So wet for me, Daisy," he smacks my bum again and then rubs it with his hand. "Do you like it when I do this?" but he doesn't wait for my response. He pushes into me to the hilt, and I groan. When he first pushes inside of me like this, I am almost ready to explode. The pain with the ecstasy. The rough and the smooth. His pace is fast and relentless. All I can hear are our moans and the slap of his balls against me. He smacks my bum again whilst he pushes deeper and harder. There's no rhythm, I can't keep up before I am exploding and moaning out his name, chasing my pleasure high. That is enough for Taron, as a few seconds later, he's chasing his own.

He stills and sighs with contentment, placing a soft kiss on my spine. He pulls out and walks over to the bathroom, I pull my dress back on. When he emerges a few moments later, I can't wait any longer.

"What happened? Why is the press here?" I feel he might actually tell me what's going on.

"Your fucking boyfriend Daniel has got his 5 minutes of fame and sold his story. He's made shit up about me, you and Melissa. The press is eating it up like the best pudding in the world."

"I didn't think he would do that," I say.

Would he?

"Don't be silly, Daisy; of course, he would; everyone will sell their souls for a price, right?" his tone is emotionless, and it makes me see red.

"I'm not silly," I bark back. The past seems to creep up on me when I least expect it to; Stefan comes filtering back through; he used to call me that 'silly'. Taron looks at me in surprise at my tone, I pick up my bag. "I'm going to go," I add.

"No, Daisy!" he strides across the room and yanks the bag out of my hand. "I need you here, I need you, Daisy, don't go; I'm sorry," his voice is sincere, and his eyes look sad. He holds out his hand and leads me back to the sofa. "Let's not discuss it anymore."

We lie together, and he holds me just like I wanted when we first had sex. I snuggle into his chest, being careful to lay my weight onto his arm more than his chest, just in case. I think over the last hour and make a note to read whatever Daniel has divulged to the press. It's clear that Taron doesn't want any of my input on the matter. He's lazily tracing circles on my back with his fingertips and I can feel my eyes becoming heavier. I stifle a yawn and listen to the steady beat of Taron's heart.

"My sister is pregnant," I confess. His fingers pause for a moment and then carry on the circles.

"That's nice," he responds. It makes me feel a little sad that he doesn't seem that bothered or ask any questions about it. The problem is that post-orgasmic sex always makes my head fuzzy and sleepy, but as I fall asleep in his arms, a thought lingers in my head.

Why is sex with Taron so good, but only when he's angry? That can't be a good thing, can it?

I remember - Taron

ELVIS PRESLEY - MEMORIES

Waking up with Daisy this morning has been amazing. We ate breakfast in bed, I was able to kiss all of her body from head to toe and when she took my dick in her mouth again, I didn't say no because when Daisy gives head, it feels immense. Her mouth is spectacularly talented and if this is what each morning looks like with Daisy, I like the way this relationship is going.

After I gave the press conference last night with a statement, the press seemed to back off a bit. But Daniel, when I find him, the man is going to pay. Nobody gets to say shit about me and think it's okay, especially when it's all lies.

The long shower with Daisy this morning helped to keep my simmering anger of Daniel at bay. I feel a little sad that I took all my anger out on Daisy, so when she suggests we go shopping today, I agree. I don't really like shopping, but I will go for Daisy, to show her I'm sorry. We take the car into town and go to a shop called Harrods – saying it's nice to just 'mooch' together in one place, and then we can go out for lunch.

We walk around the department store, hand in hand, and it feels easy; it feels right. I made the decision last night that I'm going to ask Melissa for a divorce. I know it will hurt her, and I am sorry that this has happened to her, to us. It has been eleven weeks since my not-so-heart attack, over ten weeks of remembering only snippets of my life and still absolutely jack shit of the rest. If this is my new normal, I have to move on with my new life, and I know it is with Daisy. She is perfect for me in so many ways I can't even begin to describe it and I can't ignore these feelings anymore. We bounce off one another, and the sex is incredible - although I have nothing to compare it with. I hadn't messaged or rang Melissa back from yesterday, but it is on my list to do today.

However, since arriving at the department store, I have started to get a full-on migraine. Since waking this morning, I have had an undertone of one. Hoping to brush it off, I took some of the pills and tried to push through it. But for the last hour, my headache has been relentless. This is nothing like the ones I have experienced before, I'm almost tempted to go home and rest. But with Daisy's infectious attitude and excitement about her sister being pregnant, I don't want to ruin her buzz of looking at baby clothes with her. I did, on the car ride over, book a last-minute appointment with the specialist.

The last few days, since I went away for those intense few days for treatment, they have been really bad. I have been having really vivid dreams, and then as soon as I wake up, they're gone - the brain fog at the moment is at its worst. I am glad I could secure an appointment in the morning. On the phone, the doctor reassured me again that this is quite normal when undergoing such intense cognitive treatment.

Normal, that's his favourite word. I might shove normal right up his bum when I see him tomorrow.

The pills I have taken have not even eased it either, which is odd, as they usually take the edge off. As we walk around the baby department, Daisy asks me what I think of another tiny outfit, but my vision begins to blur suddenly. A loud, high-pitched ringing in my ear; the room is all fuzzy and small at the same time. I am grateful when I feel Daisy's arm guide me to a nearby chair. I choke back the urge to vomit and put my head between my legs.

"Taron, can you hear me? Take steady breaths," I vaguely hear Daisy say; she seems far away. I shut my eyes tight. Trying to focus on my breathing, everything feels colourful, like a magical rainbow explosion of floating colours behind my eyes. It feels like there are loads of noises in my head screaming, getting louder and louder, and then there's silence. I feel light and a floating sensation through my body. I enjoy the quiet, the peace.

I wake up on the floor in the recovery position as everything comes back into focus: the light, the songs from the speakers and Daisy. I feel groggy, as if I have been woken from a nap. I rub my head, which aches, but the migraine has gone.

"How long was I out?" I ask as I go to sit up. I look at Daisy, who smiles kindly and urges me to lie back down.

"Less than a minute. Are you okay? I have called an ambulance. Try not to move," Daisy's voice is soothing, and she holds my hand, rubbing circles on it. I bolt upright because a train crash of memories smashes into my brain; I remember, I remember everything.

"Taron, are you okay? You look scared? The ambulance is like 5 minutes away; try to lie back down," she states.

"Oh shit," I say.

"What? Taron, you're scaring me," she admits.

"I remember, Daisy, I remember everything."

"That's great!" She looks so happy; her eyes are alight, but then she sees my face, and hers falls into a frown.

"No, no, it is not," I admit sadly. "I have to go, Daisy; I'm really sorry." I stand up, a little dizzy; I hold my hand against the chair and steady myself. Daisy comes to my aid, but I swot her away.

I can't have her near me, not when I know everything now.

"Okay, let me pay for this, and I will-" I put my hand on hers to show her I'm sorry, to show her that she can't follow.

"No, Daisy, *you* stay here," I say in the coldest way I can; the words make her shudder as a flash of hurt crosses her face. There goes another fucking person I have hurt, "I have to go...*alone*."

What do I do? Daisy

TAYLOR SWIFT – COME BACK... BE HERE

No, seriously, what do I do?

I watch as Taron walks away, feeling hurt. The way he spoke to me brought back the memory of being in the car with Stefan, the way that he spoke to me like a child, Taron did the same.

Chapter 35 - I have to let you go

♥

The Winter Novella – https://mybook.to/ISAYk

Trinity: For as long as I remember, I have been in love with my best friend from university. He doesn't see me. He's always been in love with the unobtainable girl. Why am I wasting my time on someone who only thinks of me as a friend when all I want to do is make love to his face with my tongue and rip his clothes off?

Send help!

Adam: As I watched the girl I have hopelessly been in love with since university get married, the love I have inside died. From now on, no woman will ever tempt me. What a fucking waste of four years of my life. I was the nice guy, the one who listened, the one who was patient, well, not anymore!

Nice guys finish last!

I'm now a man who will sleep with you once and never call you back; no one will ever ruin me again!

Find out what happens in Trinity and Adam's story, 'I Have to Let You Go', a Winter Novella, out November 2023.

~

Let's be friends!

Don't forget to follow me on Instagram: https://www.instagram.com/hb_publishing_house

Don't forget to follow me on Facebook: https://www.facebook.com/hbpublishinghouse

Don't forget to follow me on TikTok: https://www.tiktok.com/@hbpublishinghouse

Like and subscribe to my story page on YouTube: https://www.youtube.com/@timeforastory

Visit: www.hbpublishinghouse.co.uk

Acknowledgements

I loved writing about Taron and Daisy, it was so nice to actually hear Daisy's side of everything that happened and what her struggles are. I honestly thought Taron was the one and what an interesting twist he wasn't. Halfway through this story, I sat down with Sarah and she just said, he isn't for Daisy, I wonder what he will do when he remembers!? So, you will have to wait and see what happens - sorry for the cliffhanger; I just love them so much – blame Lisa for that.

To Anna, you are awesome proofreaders and thank you for saving me again! To Paige for bringing me into the modern world and writing the playlists for the book. Lisa, thanks for encouraging me and helping me with this one, I think I have cried far too many times over this book. Hajni, thank you for being my cheerleader! And Charlene, you strong ninja, I made my promise not to give you any more spoilers – but I can't promise I will for the next book.

To my family for letting me have the time to write this; my girls are the best, I hope that they grow up and love books as much as me!

Thank you for reading this book, I hope you love it as much as I did when I wrote it.

The Playlist

Chapter 1: Dolly Patron – 9 to 5 https://open.spotify.com/track/4w3tQBXhn5345eUXDGBWZG

Chapter 2: Lykke Li - sex money feelings die https://open.spotify.com/track/0g4fzRkbLeCDUCoe5iUOcf

Chapter 3: Evanescence – Bring Me To Life https://open.spotify.com/track/0COqiPhxzoWICwFCS4eZcp

Chapter 4: SYML – Where's My Love https://open.spotify.com/track/1B62o4CbdL9ckGvwsz2cgn

Chapter 5: Sofia Carson - Come Back Home https://open.spotify.com/track/1I4dwH7C0jBAEtz5DjlJgQ

Chapter 6: Ruth B. - Lost Boy https://open.spotify.com/track/0zMzy-HAeMvwq5CRstru1Fp

Chapter 7: Vance Joy - Who Am I https://open.spotify.com/track/6Is6Wxw0iivqDIQmlFeG6F

Chapter 8: Pitbull - Time Of Our Lives https://open.spotify.com/track/2bJvl42r8EF3wxjOuDav4r

Chapter 9: Blackbear - idfc https://open.spotify.com/track/3SErMoIKdRELto2OspGs5L

Chapter 10: Ariana Grande – needy https://open.spotify.com/track/1TEL6MISSVLSdhOSddidlJ

Chapter 11: Jennifer Lopez - Let's Get Loud https://open.spotify.com/track/6kQz6t5z1FK4uohPh8Kd73

Chapter 12: Coldplay - Yellow https://open.spotify.com/track/3AJwUDP919kvQ9QcozQPxg

Chapter 13: Mumford & Sons - Little Lion Man https://open.spotify.com/track/3QjpO5xOB9ErJ95AxT0h0r

Chapter 14: Tom Odell - Heal https://open.spotify.com/track/4KlL5Bwlm4yHYxr0B2rHc

Chapter 15: Bruno Mars – Halo https://open.spotify.com/track/6SKwQg hsR8AISIxhcwyA9R

Chapter 16: Beyonce - Halo https://open.spotify.com/track/2CvOqDpQI Mw69cCzWqr5yr

Chapter 17: The Weeknd - Call Out My Name https://open.spotify.com/ track/5YnKnnckD0Rid9Fib5vQY5

Chapter 18: Rihanna - Shut Up And Drive https://open.spotify.com/trac k/7AQjiRtIpr33P8UT98iveh

Chapter 19: James Bay - Let It Go https://open.spotify.com/track/40EB7 ABUO6MoWMUwPKptJ7

Chapter 20: Bea Miller - Feel Something https://open.spotify.com/track /7JDWhC422Gtk1Bq0mL3OTC

Chapter 21: Lauv - The Story Never Ends https://open.spotify.com/trac k/2hTcD5aTYlQoTT76KofQam

Chapter 22: Sia - Helium https://open.spotify.com/track/4S6fv0puLCsfY jyBTPDb9k

Chapter 23: Take That - Babe https://open.spotify.com/track/3jGTua1b rraVUrUOioMqLS

Chapter 24: Ed Sheeran - Remember The Name https://open.spotify.co m/track/0AtP8EkGPn6SwxKDaUuXec

Chapter 25:   One Direction - Little Things https://open.spoti- fy.com/track/0TAmnCzOtqRfvA38DDLTjj

Chapter 26: Arctic Monkeys - I Wanna Be Yours https://open.spotify.co m/track/5XeFesFbtLpXzIVDNQP22n

Chapter 27: Gesaffelstein & The Weeknd - Lost in the Fire https://open. spotify.com/track/2vXKRlJBXyOcvZYTdNeckS

Chapter 28: The Neighbourhood - Daddy Issues https://open.spotify.co m/track/5E30LdtzQTGqRvNd7l6kG5

Chapter 29: Chase Atlantic - Friends https://open.spotify.com/track/7Ll LABogx8SHeMPJbLBvBH

Chapter 30: Alec Benjamin - If We Have Each Other https://open.spoti-fy.com/track/7pT6WSg4PCt4mr5ZFyUfsF

Chapter 31: Panic! At The Disco - Ready to Go https://open.spotify.com /track/7m4HUtdXRUHEitLlqbVWxf

Chapter 32: Olivia Rodrigo - 1 step forward, 3 steps back https://open.s potify.com/track/3EhtBGP8MRtYRJhR4QYDdP

Chapter 33: Elvis Presley Memories https://open.spotify.com/track/6jG zInaZ1QyKLNw61an9y5

Chapter 34: Taylor Swift - Come Back... Be Here https://open.spotify.co m/track/4pNApnaUWAL2J4KO2eqokq

Printed in Great Britain
by Amazon

31957027R00106